Also by Jan Springer

Cowboys Online
Cowboys for Christmas
Cowboys In Her Pocket
Loving Her Cowboys
Cowboys in Her Heart
Always Her Cowboys

Intimate Secrets
Intimate Lover
Intimate Kisses

Kidnap Fantasies
Jade's Fantasy
Zero To Sexy
Christmas Lovers

Pleasure Bound
A Hero's Welcome

A Hero Escapes
A Hero Betrayed
A Hero's Kiss
A Hero Wanted
Captive Heroes

Pleasure Bound Boxed Set

Pleasure Bound : COMPLETE SERIES SciFi Erotic Romance Boxed Set

Tentacles Shifter Erotic Romance

Taken by Him

The Key Club

A Merry Menage Christmas
Sophie's Menage
Jewel's Menage
Jaxie's Menage
A Homecoming Menage Christmas

The Outlaw Lovers

Jude
The Claiming
Colter's Revenge
Tyler's Woman
Resistance

The Outlaw Lovers
Alpha Outlaws Boxed Set

Vampira
Sweet Heat
Wet Heat
Crimson Heat

Standalone
A Touch of Menage Boxed Set
Shades of Menage Boxed Set
Naughty Girl Desires Boxed Set
Nice Girl Naughty
Sinderella Sexy
The Biker and The Bride
The Fire Within
Bared to Him
Pleasure Bound : A Futuristic Adult Romance Boxed Set
Merry Menage Kisses Boxed Set
Stripped Naked
Risqué Girl Delights Boxed Set
A Holiday Menage
Ménage À Trois
A Hitman for Hannah
Billionaire Boyfriend

Watch for more at www.janspringer.com.

Hannah Roberts is a clone, a breeding Slave designed solely for the purpose of producing healthy offspring for an ailing human race. But she longs for the forbidden—her freedom and the dangerous man she can never have. With her breeding status about to commence, Hannah escapes her captors and is on the run for her life.

Trained to be a cold-blooded killing machine, the only light in Jacob Romero's life is a beautiful Slave whose sweet innocence brands his heart and awakens dark desires he never knew he had. Assigned to hunt her down and kill her, he's seriously injured when he instead saves her life.

Now they are fugitives from the only world they've ever known and Hannah nurses the wounded Hitman she's always wanted. Soon their attraction ignites into a fire neither can deny. But their forbidden love will face one final challenge as they prepare to escape into a harsh new life in the Free States.

A Hitman for Hannah

Published by Spunky Girl Publishing

Copyright 2002, 2008, 2017 Jan Springer

3rd edition

Edited by Zara Kelly

Cover Art by Talina Perkins ~ Bookin' It Designs

License Notes

This ebook is licensed for your personal use only.

Author Note

This is a work of fiction. Characters, places, settings and events presented in this book are purely of the author's imagination and bear no resemblance to any actual person, living or dead or to any actual events, places and/or settings.

Glossary

ENHANCED EYES: Infrared heat-seeking lenses embedded into the eyes and wired to the brain of Hitmen and Hitwomen drafted into the Hit Association.

enhanced hearing: Electrical implants embedded into the ears and wired to the brain. The unit enhances a Hitman's or Hitwoman's hearing.

tazer gun: Sends out green ray probes of electricity and shocks the intended victim into unconsciousness.

laser gun: Depending upon the strength of the ray, it can either severely burn or kill the intended victim. In most cases it is used on a runner.

runner: A Breeding Slave or Breeding Stud who decides the breeding life is not for him or her and runs for the Free States.

Breeder Slave or Stud: Designer babies produced specifically to be conditioned into being Breeders. As adults they will be paired with mates to create healthy babies for the ailing human race.

Free States: A harsh, lawless, cold land north of the States border where runners gain their freedom. They must survive here using their wits.

States: Since Armageddon the States have been run by a harsh dictatorship government that is trying to repopulate the land with a superior race of humans. It uses any means necessary to accomplish its goals.

Hitman or Hitwoman: Men and women drafted into the Hit Association. Their draft is for life or death, whichever comes first.

Hit Association: A group of men and women drafted and trained to hunt down runners. They are given enhanced eyes and ears and other equipment to assist them in their jobs.

Armageddon Time: In the year 2050 A.C. the Fourth World War begins. It began with a conflict between the U.S. and North Korea and over the years the entire world is involved. The World War rages for seven long years. After a rain of nuclear bombs completes the war, the ensuing pollution gives the world an ailing civilization that clings to the hope of a future using genetically designed healthy Breeding Slaves and Studs—Clones, designer babies, Copies—to produce offspring for them.

Forward

Year 50 A.A. (50 years After Armageddon)

DUE TO THE ARMAGEDDON Time, radiation and pollution continue to plague the Earth. Cancers and other diseases, stem cell research and organ transplants are common. Treatments of the diseases are often extreme, leaving many with side effects such as sterility. Human reproductive failures are at epidemic proportions. The human race begins to shrink. If nothing is done, human will eventually face extinction.

Cloning from quality, radiation-resistant embryos becomes the norm, allowing non-reproductive couples to have access to healthy test-tube babies. However, studies reveal such babies aren't as resilient to pollution or radiation as those conceived in a human host. Couples demand access to healthier children.

Clones, as they were known in the A.C.—After Christ—years, are now created in massive quantities in the A.A. Called Copies or designer babies, they have been genetically manipulated to produce superior-quality offspring and their sole purpose in life is to be Breeding Slaves or Studs. Only the rich, childless humans are eligible for the enhanced offspring of the Breeder Slaves. These superior babies will be integrated into society.

After a conditioning period of eighteen years, the Breeder Slaves and Studs are moved to privately owned breeding farms—a very lucrative business where a rich couple will pay quite handsomely to purchase a baby and watch their child's creation from conception to birth by the two Copies they select.

However certain factions protest the use of clones for breeding purposes. It goes against human morals, they say. Copies are just as human as the rest of the people. They bleed blood, they understand and have emotions. They should be free to live in society as the rest of the humans. They should have the right to pick their mates, have their own children. To gain an education.

Activists fight for Breeder Slave and Stud rights. The government listens—to an extent. Strict rights are granted. Copies are educated. Female Copies are allowed to keep their firstborn until the child is eighteen when a master can either sell the firstborn as a Breeder Slave or set him or her free.

Then there are the downfalls. Being a Breeding Slave must remain a life sentence. It is, after all, why these enhanced humans have been created. To serve mankind. There can be no marriage between Breeder Slave and Stud or humans. If a Slave or Stud runs, he or she must pay a deadly consequence.

Elimination.

Hannah is a Breeding Slave and she's running. Jacob is the Hitman assigned to eliminate her.

Neither has known passion or love.

Until now.

Prologue

Earth—the States
Six weeks earlier

"YOU HAVE SUCH A TIGHT ass, my Hannah."

Twenty-one year-old Hannah Roberts inhaled sharply as the hard tip of Simon's lubricated shaft stretched her tender anal muscles.

Warmth draped against her back as his hot hands reached around her to tenderly clasp on the nipple clamps he insisted she wear on the nights he bedded her.

The clamps pinched a little, but when he switched on the vibrator, her nipples responded quickly and tightened into hard, aching beads.

With his cock buried inside her ass, he slowly bent her upper body forward over the padded barstool, allowing her breasts to dangle.

"I've got a surprise for you, my darling Hannah," he whispered. "Tonight will be our last night together."

She couldn't help but breathe a little sigh of relief. Being Simon's play toy for almost four years was a bore, but the alternative of producing babies, made him tolerable. He had her on the monthly birth control shot, made her wear vibrating nipple clamps, butt plugs, and because he had an anal fetish, he only did anal on her. Her joy of knowing tonight would be their last night, however, was short-lived.

"In a couple of months you'll be twenty-two years old. I know you were eligible for being a Breeding Slave when I first purchased you at eighteen, and I admit I've been selfish by keeping you all to myself, and not allowing you your first-born, but something special happened today. A very influential and rich young couple engaged to be married dropped by the plantation. Both of them are sterile due to their cancer treatments and tests show she is unable to carry a child to term even

9

if she has artificial insemination. They are looking for the parents for their first child.

"They saw you, Hannah. They fell in love with your flawless skin and sweet looks. I told them your health record is impeccable. That you were created with natural immunity to cancers as well as immunity to respiratory illnesses, and that with the perfectly selected mate you would produce healthy children for them. They were impressed. They told me they wish to go the route of watching their child being conceived when the time comes for you to be paired with the father. Hannah, they picked Judias to father their child. But because of the law, we need to have you impregnated immediately with your first-born. Then you are free to bear their children as well. They want at least six children of their own and they are extremely rich."

Hannah tried hard not to tense at his words.

Having Judias to father a child, let alone many, was a compliment to a Breeder Slave. He was the plantation's best Stud, but she was afraid of him. She'd seen him in the shower stalls on several occasions when she was on clean-up duty. Had watched him perform sex on the selected Breeding Slaves during the Ceremonies. When he was aroused he was too big and many Breeding Slaves were injured during penetration because of his size.

Sex with him was said to be painful and short. Sometimes impregnation occurred in only one session. It seemed the pain and injury to his assets were worth it for Simon as the babes Judias bore a Breeder Slave were magnificent. They were healthy, robust and perfect. Everything the human parents wanted. Despite that, she didn't want to be fucked by him.

She had no feelings for him. Only fear. Although she knew she must do as Simon instructed and bear children, she also wanted more than just sex and popping out babies.

She wanted what she could never have. Freedom and love.

Simon must have noticed her tenseness because his next words were softly spoken.

"Shhh, darling. I've signed the contract and it is best we get started right away with the firs-born so you'll be ready to go at it with Judias shortly after the birth. That's why I've decided tomorrow will be the first day of your Breeding Ceremony."

Breeding Ceremony. The two words burned horror through Hannah.

Simon Walker was a small but growing number of masters who gave their Breeding Slaves this Ceremony. Virgin females were given gorgeous red dresses signifying they would soon become first-time mothers. The red dress was worn throughout the Ceremony until she was pregnant. In many cases, sex sessions to conceive a first-born would be open for viewing in front of the Breeder Slaves and others. It was, in her opinion, a cheap, crude form of entertainment.

"How wonderful!"

She forced her voice to remain lively and upbeat, the way her teachers taught during her conditioning years. They had instructed her to follow every order from a master just as every good submissive Slave should. They told her she was part of the Human Enhancement Programme. She was a designer baby. A transhuman. Translation—a Clone. A Copy created for the sole purpose of being breeding stock for humans. It was the government's plan to eventually replace regular humans with a superior race, the transhuman. A race that would be able tolerate the pollution and diseases regular humans carried.

Inhaling slowly, she forced herself to keep calm. She needed to stay relaxed and be submissive.

She knew that with any significant sign of defiance she would be killed. She wasn't immune to Simon's wrath. Although she was a valuable asset as well as a plaything to be used by him, he would punish her if she disobeyed his orders. He took extreme pride in his pristine reputation for producing excellent healthy babies and having the best quality of obedient slaves. She'd watched him whip an older Breeder Slave to within an inch of her life for an infraction as simple as saying she wasn't feeling well enough to have sex with a selected Stud on a particular day. A few months later that same Slave died in Hannah's arms after a very hard birth. The child had died days later.

Her guts churned in anxiety at the thought of being dressed in the traditional ceremonial gown and secured like a trapped farm cow in the breeding barn. Having people watch as she lay on a padded table, her legs held tight in stirrups while Judias penetrated her, emptying his valuable seed inside her. Or having her body bent at the waist over a cushioned bar, much as she was now, her pussy exposed so Judias could have sex with her until she became pregnant.

No. She couldn't do this.

"I've picked out several Ceremonial gowns for the Breeding Ceremony. Of course they are the traditional red coloring, but they are made of the finest, softest see-through silk. Only the best for my prettiest Copy. And since the contract states the couple wants the children of theirs to be exclusively between you and Judias, your firstborn will have to be fathered by someone else. I've decided I will give all six of my sister's sons equal opportunity to bed you. I am sure they were all very pleased to hear the news, especially Jacob."

At the mention of Jacob Romero, Simon's sister's eldest son, Hannah's heart picked up speed.

"I sent him a message too, letting him know about your Ceremony."

"He's coming here?" She couldn't help but show her enthusiasm.

"He's coming here."

Hannah inhaled softly.

She longed to see the eldest Romero brother again. Jacob was ten years her senior and on occasion he came to visit his Uncle Simon.

Although he was a Hitman and an enemy of Breeder Slaves, he always dropped by the quarters to visit with the slaves that Jacob and his brothers had grown up with when they'd spent school summer vacations here at his uncle's breeding plantation. According to the slaves, Jacob was more of a friend than a killer and it had been the worst day of their lives when they heard the government drafted him into becoming a Hitman. Rumors continued to circulate it was his own father who'd instigated the draft, hoping to harden his tenderhearted son.

Despite being a cold-blooded killer, Jacob looked at her with such carnal yearning in his eyes she always felt hot and aroused, wishing he would sneak into her quarters at night. But he never did. Yet she fantasized about him endlessly. Every time she saw him her infatuation for him grew, yet he was never anything but a gentleman to her, leading her to believe he would follow the government rules without exception.

She was a Copy. Created for the sole purpose to be a Breeder Slave.

He was a Hitman, a hunter of Breeder Slaves and Studs. He was her enemy.

There was no chance for them to be together. Ever. Yet she still fantasized and hoped that one day things would change in today's society, allowing her to pursue him and make him her man. Instinct told her Jacob should have been the only man for her. Should have been the only father for her children.

Secretly, as far as she was concerned, she was a woman. A woman who wanted Jacob. Just thinking of him sent a familiar hum shifting through her.

Suddenly she wanted to look upon his handsome face again. To have his powerful muscles flex beneath her fingertips as she clenched his broad back. To feel his hard thighs cradle her hips as he plunged his shaft into her. The thought of seeing him again made her insides ignite with a want so compelling she almost cried out at its intensity.

"I look forward to seeing him," she whispered.

Simon withdrew his cock and plunged into her again, making her gasp at the ruthless intrusion. She sensed he'd become angry when speaking about Jacob.

"I know my nephew wants you, Hannah," he said between gritted teeth. "I see the way he looks at you. Perhaps I should only allow the two of you to be paired for the firstborn as he has previously requested, but he needs to see you for what you are. Allowing him to fuck you will put him at peace. Knowing his five brothers have also been with you and not knowing which fathered your child should put his infatuation for you to rest. He needs to know you were created for the sole purpose of being a Breeding Slave, a Copy, not someone fit to marry."

Jacob had requested to be the father of her firstborn? Simon had refused? His denial of Jacob for her mate hurt like a blade striking deep into her heart, but she remained quiet.

"It's too bad I'm sterile or I would have impregnated you with your firstborn myself."

The urge to tell him she was not as stupid as the other Breeding Slaves in hanging around and becoming pregnant year after year so he could profit from her babies was so great she almost said it out loud, but his hard cock was sliding back out of her ass and she forced herself to relax yet again.

Past experience taught her that Simon loved to fuck hard and fast. If she kept herself relaxed and he finished quickly, it would leave her plenty of time to put her plan into motion.

"I'm sure my six nephews will go easy on you."

"The more the merrier," she said in as light a voice as she could create. She tried to forget the fact he had just told her he expected her to be shared with all the Romero brothers, not just Jacob, which she would have preferred.

"I know six men is a handful for your Ceremony. It'll be quite a show to watch you and my nephews together. Not to mention the other Slaves will be quite entertained."

She inhaled sharply as his hot fingers spread her labia in order to stroke her clit.

"You and the Romero brothers will produce such a beautiful child, I have no doubt. And of course, as tradition dictates, your firstborn will be yours to keep until he or she is eighteen and then I can profit off he or she for the trouble of caring for them. Rest assured your first-born will have the same kept life as you. No worries about anything. Most would kill to be in your shoes."

For the first time in a long while Hannah smiled.

But it was bittersweet.

She would never allow a child of hers to become a pawn of the government or Simon. And she would never have the opportunity of finding out if those rumors about Jacob being an excellent lover were true.

Because tonight she was leaving. Tonight she was going to run.

Chapter One

Six weeks later

HER PUSSY WAS TIGHT. Damn tight. And damn hot as Jacob Romero slid in and out of her in an achingly sensual rhythm. Beneath him, Hannah moaned, her body shuddered as she enjoyed what he was doing to her.

He knew she'd be like this. Knew she'd be the one woman for him.

He thrust harder into her. Deeper. Her cries of passion rang like music in his ears.

The pressure inside his penis mounted. He was going to come soon. The moist heat of her vaginal muscles spasmed around his thick flesh, welcoming him in, sending shards of lightning zipping up his shaft straight into his belly.

Oh yes! He was going to come.

Clenching his jaw, he shuddered and released his hot semen deep into her very core...

The screeching sound of a seagull's cry ripped Jacob Romero from his erotic fantasy.

He blinked at the softness of the ocean wind caressing his face. Listened to the waves as they roared onto the sand-rippled beach. For a moment he was lost in the natural beauty. The reason for his being here totally forgotten.

He shielded his eyes from the blazing sun as it dipped to the horizon, casting a golden hue over the sexy black-haired woman.

Hannah Roberts.

A Copy.

Breeding Slave.

Runner.

She stood on the beach. Not more than twenty feet away from him.

It was a crime she looked so good in clothes. A bigger crime that he'd been the one sent to kill her.

Jacob grit his teeth in sudden anger. Over the years as a Hitman he never thought about not doing what he'd been trained for. Runners were killed. It was as simple as that. If one were allowed to go free, then they would all want to go free. But now, as he looked at his sweet Hannah, he couldn't stop the aching weariness sweeping over him. A weariness that made him realize he was sick and tired of killing.

He wanted out of this nightmare job.

Unfortunately, there was no way out. Once drafted, the job was for life. He hadn't been given a choice. Hadn't been allowed to follow his yearnings in life.

And one of those yearnings had been taking Hannah for his very own.

His gaze drew back to her. To her long hair flying in the salty breeze.

Her tank top hugged generous breasts. White shorts revealed wide hips and long legs. Ocean waves lapped at her bare feet.

He wondered what her toes would taste like. Marveled at how smooth those legs would feel against his lips as he planted tiny kisses along her flesh until he finally nestled his face between her legs to suckle her sweet clit.

Her laughter broke into his thoughts.

She watched a white seagull soar over her head. Her amusement was unbelievably beautiful. The sound of her pleasure crashed through his enhanced hearing and cracked the iciness lining his heart.

For a split second he almost turned around. Almost left her there. Almost let her go free.

But he couldn't do it. He couldn't let her get away. Slowly he lifted the laser gun.

Inhaling a deep, shuddering breath, he pressed the butt of the weapon hard against the crook of his shoulder. He took a bead on Hannah and his trembling finger tightened on the firing button.

HANNAH ROBERTS COULDN'T stop laughing. She was absolutely delirious with happiness. Soon she'd be picked up by a boat and whisked away north of the border. To a land the Breeding Slaves called the Free States. The impatience of waiting for someone to contact her had just about driven her crazy.

Hugging the tiny communicator to her breasts, she remembered the whispery voice of the man who'd called early this morning, instructing her to come down to the beach late afternoon and that she would be picked up by nightfall. He'd sounded kind and gentle and extremely mysterious. Nonetheless, at this point in time she was desperate. She was almost out of food and quite anxious to get a new start in life.

Although she was surprised to discover how beautiful it was out here by the ocean, free from the polluted yellow haze surrounding the breeder farm, she couldn't wait to inhale freedom's air. Couldn't wait to start living life on *her* terms.

Freedom was mere days away from their plantation according to the whispered words of a dying Breeding Slave she and her best friend Lara had tended several months ago after the Slave had suffered complications from a difficult birth.

All they had to do was be brave enough to escape, the Slave had said.

But they must tell no one, the Slave instructed. No one must know of the windmill with the nearby abandoned stone beach mansion as being a contact place for the Underground Railroad who helped slaves escape their captors. For if they were fool enough to tell of this place then many lives would be in peril.

All they would have to do, she'd said, was find the ocean and follow the coastline to the tiny fishing village of Crag Rock. About another day's walk north along the shore there would be an old rusty windmill on a hill with an abandoned stone mansion nearby. Stay there, keep out of sight and wait.

They will come for you, she'd said. *They will come and take you to the Free States. To freedom.* Then the slave, racked with pain, had sucked in her last ragged breath and died.

Her best friend Lara thought the Slave was delirious from the fever and never mentioned what the woman said again. Hannah, however, kept to the hope that maybe the Slave had been telling the truth.

And it appeared she had.

She had stolen an electric car from Simon's barn and after only one night of driving west, Hannah found the ocean. She'd hidden the vehicle beneath some brush at the end of an old rutted road that looked as if it had not seen a car in years. With luck, no one would find the vehicle for a very long time.

Then, wearing the large knapsack that contained nonperishable foods that she had stolen from the main house and stored in an upstairs loft of one of the barns on the plantation, she had then followed the rocky coastline north.

She traveled by night and slept by day hidden in bushes. A week later, she skirted the village of Crag Rock. A day after that, she spied the windmill silhouetted in the blue splash of moonlight. It was an eerie figure against the backdrop of the black night sky and sent shivers coursing up and down her back. When she saw the abandoned mansion, her breath had come so quickly, a weird headiness had embraced her as she ran up to the house.

For five long weeks she had waited here for contact, her anxiety mounting every day. Early this morning her heart had burst with both excitement and fear when she found the communicator on the back porch. An hour later, she received the call.

Nobody would ever tell her what to do again and no man would be allowed to screw her any time he wished. She should have made the escape sooner. But she'd been afraid of leaving the safety of the plantation. Her fear of being paired with Judias was stronger and she'd fled, risking her life.

Another fierce gust whipped against her, making her stumble backward. Making her smile into the hot sunshine as the warm sand grains sifted through her naked toes.

Six weeks ago, when she'd first escaped, she would never have imagine how beautiful freedom would feel. How perfectly scary it would be to stand on an ocean beach in northern Oregon waiting to rendezvous with the Underground Railroad.

Six weeks ago, her owner, Simon, was doing whatever he wanted to her. His lecherous hands fondling her aroused clit as he pushed himself into her ass and informing her she would have to have sex with a man she feared. Even the thought of finally being with Jacob before being with Judias hadn't stopped her from running.

Thankfully those days were gone.

With the dying Slave's whispered directions etched in Hannah's brain and her heart heavy for leaving her pregnant friend behind without so much as asking her if she wanted to come too, she'd escaped. Thanks to her education, she knew how to read a map. Thanks to one of her jobs as a tractor driver in the plantation fields, she knew how to keep an electric car charged via the various free charging stations and she knew how to drive. It made the escape much easier.

Doubt and questions had plagued her during her stay here.

Perhaps it had just been the fever screwing with the dying Breeder Slave's mind as Lara had thought? Perhaps no one would come for her? If the Slave had known this house was a contact spot for the Underground Railroad, then why hadn't she run when she found out about it? Unless it had just been a dream of hers? No, it couldn't be a dream. The house was here. The rusty windmill too. Just as the Slave described it.

So why weren't other Slaves using this place?

Although deserted, the stone mansion with the faded aqua shutters and the long octagonal window in the attic did show signs of use. In the one-room attic she'd found a large bed with a reasonably new mattress. She'd washed sheets she found in a closet. Discovered a used bar of flower-scented soap down by the beach and used it to wash the linens in the ocean and used it to keep herself spotless. She needed to make a good impression for when she was rescued.

The kitchen floor had looked as if it had been recently swept clean too. And out the back porch, down by the beach, were the remnants of a fire, possibly used for cooking.

This morning she'd been out in the ocean, fishing, using a sharpened stick as a spear. When she came back without success in catching her breakfast, she'd found the communicator on the back veranda in plain sight. Beneath it, a white note fluttered in the breeze.

Don't be afraid. I will call.

And he had.

Now she was here. Standing at the arranged rendezvous point, waiting to be taken to freedom.

She was leaving everything behind. The knapsack, her change of clothes, what little she had left of the food, everything. It was all stashed in the attic room. Whoever came after her would inherit her belongings, if they found them.

She was leaving everything because she didn't want to be reminded of this life. She needed a fresh start. A new beginning.

"Hannah." The sound of a familiar masculine voice ripped her from her thoughts, and for several frozen seconds Hannah could do nothing but stand with paralyzed fear as her brain tried to decipher the fact she'd been caught.

Caught by Jacob. The only man she'd ever wanted.

Jacob. The one man she'd never expected to see again in her life.

Her newfound peace crashed in around her.

"Sweet mercy! No!" she heard herself whisper.

"Do as I say and everything will be fine," he said from immediately behind her.

Her heart crashed against her chest. She clamped down on the hysteria threatening to engulf her.

"Turn around. Nice and slow," he instructed.

Hannah didn't know if she could do it. Dizziness swirled, making her unsteady. The communicator she held dropped from her hand.

She didn't know how, but she managed to turn.

Her breath seized in her lungs at the sight of him. She'd missed him so much it hurt just to look at him.

He was taller than she remembered. Wider in the shoulders. His usually clean-cut appearance was anything but. Dark stubble etched his chin, his upper lip, the sides of his full mouth. His brown hair looked windblown and longer than she remembered, curling over his ears and at the base of his neck. He looked dangerous, sweet and sexy all rolled into one.

She *wanted* him to be her ally, her man, her lover. Wanted it so badly she almost reached out to curl her arms around his neck. Almost asked him to run away with her, but when she saw his eyes, she froze. The familiar sparkle he'd always toted for her when he looked at her in the past was gone, replaced by the deadest, darkest blue eyes she'd ever seen.

And he pointed a laser gun directly at her heart.

Her hold on sanity began to slip.

No! Was he really going to kill her?

Trembling panic slammed into her legs, her arms, and the rest of her.

"Please don't make this difficult," Jacob said. His voice sounded cold and emotionless.

He's going to kill me! She took a step backward as horror raged through her. She barely felt the warm ocean water swirl around her ankles.

His frown deepened.

She winced and cried out as he suddenly grabbed her arm, jerking her against his muscular body.

"Why did you run, Hannah?" he growled. Anger seared through his voice and a tortured look of betrayal flooded his eyes as he glared at her. Suddenly she wondered if the sweet, gentle Jacob she'd fantasized about had been just that. A fantasy. Did reality stand in front of her? Reality being a cold, angry man?

A Hitman.

A man she could not trust.

The thought frightened her. Fear boiled through her with such ferocity, with such insane intensity, that before she knew what she was doing, she slammed the palm of her hand under and up against his chin.

The defensive maneuver she'd once secretly been taught by a fellow female slave worked.

He groaned in surprise and his tight grasp loosened enough to allow herself to wrench free.

In a split second she was running down the beach. There was no way she would die this close to freedom. No way! From behind her, Jacob yelled at her to stop.

In defiance, her legs moved faster. The thought of him shooting her in the back urged her to change directions every few seconds. Forced her to falter over the sharp rocks and to ignore the pain sparking into the tender bottoms of her bare feet. She skirted the sand dunes and headed toward a rutted road she knew was up ahead. A road she'd explored during her time here and knew it would lead to a highway two miles away. Maybe someone would help her? Unfortunately the terrain only became rougher. The rocks turned into small boulders that were hidden by tall clumps of dry yellow grass.

She skirted around a rock but managed to stub her toe on something hard. Pain lanced up her foot into her leg. She bit back a cry, pushed aside the agony and kept her feet pounding the ground.

Her lungs began to burn, her leg muscles cramped, but the pain was nothing compared to being killed by the man she'd fantasized about and thought she'd loved. That thought made her run even faster, if that was possible.

She was running at a dangerous pace. Anything could happen. She could hit another boulder, stick her foot into a hole, break a leg...

She could hear his heaving breath behind her. Could hear the way his shoes crushed the hard, dry earth.

He was gaining on her! Cold perspiration prickled her body. She could almost feel his hot breath on the back of her neck. Could feel his body heat slam into her flesh.

Sensing he was about to tackle her, she turned abruptly and headed west back toward the beach. She would dive into the ocean. Swim to freedom if she had to.

Behind her, he cursed.

Before long, the soothing warm sand sifted beneath her feet. The ocean sparkled with welcome thirty feet away. Then twenty.

She began to pray as never before. Prayed he would give up. Prayed he would simply let her go.

Her prayers went unanswered.

An instant later, a strong hand grabbed her by the elbow, making her whirl around. She lost her balance and fell.

He came down on her like a sack of potatoes, wiping the wind out of her burning lungs.

She couldn't move. Couldn't breathe. Couldn't gather her senses.

He lay on top of her, his hot breath wheezing over her face like painful knife blades. His muscular length crushed her into the ground. And his cold blue eyes glared angrily into her very soul.

"It's over, Hannah. It's over," he breathed.

Over? The word took a good fifteen seconds to register, before it made sense.

It couldn't be over. Not like this. Not here. Not when she was so close to freedom.

She searched her mind frantically for a way out. A way to save herself.

"You can't kill me! You can't! I love you!" Hysteria made her weak. Made her confess. Through her panic, she spied something powerful flash in his eyes.

Was it sympathy? Confusion?

No.

It was desire. Dark and dangerous desire. The passion in his gaze stunned her. Frightened her. Excited her.

Air ebbed back into her lungs.

Along with her breath came her senses.

All of her senses.

He smelled like her man, her refuge, her rescuer. She had a desperate need to lose herself in those hopeful thoughts or she would go mad with the alternative thought of death.

She needed to lose herself in the only thing that felt right at the moment. Those intimate memories of her fantasies of him. Of him touching her. His hard body intimately on top of hers. Maybe she was dreaming of his strong muscular thighs straddling each side of her hips, their power holding her beneath him? Dreaming this whole day?

"I've waited so long for you, Hannah. So goddamn long. And when I came to the plantation to take you, you were gone."

His eyes didn't seem dead anymore. They flashed with desire and intent. She knew she should be fighting him for her life. Begging him. Pleading.

Perhaps deep down somewhere inside her she knew he was more powerful than she. That it was useless to fight. That he wouldn't really hurt her.

The scorching way he looked at her was so intoxicating she could only acknowledge her body's response.

His powerful chest heaved against her clothing, scraping her nipples. Hardening them into two aching buds. A pure craving exploded between her legs, and when his hot mouth suddenly melted against her trembling lips, she could do nothing but submit to his seductive assault.

His mouth tasted moist, lush and full of secret promises. His lips slid over hers with a rough gentleness, which sent crisp sparks of want deep into her very core.

She whimpered as his bold tongue slid between her teeth and invaded her mouth.

Sensations bombarded her as his hot tongue explored. Instinctively, she wound her arms around his neck, pulling him closer into the intoxicating kiss.

Excitement zipped along her nerve endings, making her ache for his touch. Ache for this fantasy to be reality.

When he finally drew away from her, his face was flushed with want. The bulge pressing against her abdomen was thick and hard. It made her tremble with a carnal craving she'd never experienced before.

"I have to taste you, Hannah. I have to see if you are real."

Her heart crashed in her ears as she concentrated on what he was saying to her. Did he think this was a fantasy too?

"I promise I won't hurt you. I won't kill you. Just a taste of your sweetness. Just a taste and then we can talk."

A taste? He wanted to go down on her? He wasn't going to kill her? Relief at his words should be pouring through her. Instead she became mesmerized by the sexual heat in his eyes. She nodded.

Upon her consent, his chest lifted off hers and he slithered down between her legs. When his hot hands seared against the burning flesh of her inner thighs, reality hit and for one brief instant she panicked again.

This was *not* a fantasy!

What if he killed her afterward?

"Easy, Hannah. I won't hurt you. I promise."

His blue eyes were so dark that she could scarcely breathe. The Breeder Slaves said he was a good man. Her instincts told her he wouldn't hurt her. She had to trust her instincts. Had to trust him. She had no other choice.

She inhaled sharply as her shorts and underwear were tugged down and off her legs. She felt the warmth of the grainy sand nestle against her ass.

Hannah found herself lifting her knees and spreading her legs for him. She loved the ravenous look in his eyes. It was an expression she remembered so well.

A look he'd never acted on, until now.

But did she want him this way? Should she accept him this way?

Lying half naked on the beach where her rescuers might witness what he was about to do to her?

"Jacob—"

"You're so beautiful. Too beautiful for me," he whispered from his position between her legs. He looked drunk. Drunk with desire.

Hannah bit back a gasp as his hot fingers slid along her inner thighs toward her pussy. She jolted as his fingers parted her nether lips. The stubble on his face grazed against her inner thighs, creating a firestorm of need. His hot tongue flicked against her sensitive clit and she couldn't help but moan from his touch.

She closed her eyes and lifted her hips, pressing her aching flesh against his face. Wet heat trickled from between her legs. She'd always craved him. Desired him to be the one and only man who would ever thrust his shaft deep inside her.

With tormenting licks, he massaged her clit until her thighs were shuddering and pleasure rocked her.

"Jacob, please." Frustration gnawed at her and she dug her fingers into the warm sand.

She wanted him to fuck her. To bring her to fulfillment.

He lifted his head and the drunken look of desire made her heart sing with joy. She just *knew* she was safe with him.

"You taste even better than I ever imagined, Hannah. So much sweeter."

Once again he dipped his head between her legs.

She jerked as he sucked and sipped. His hot mouth brought her to the edge of a precipice she ached to descend into, and just when she was about to freefall, he backed off, leaving her gasping for air and her body unbelievably tense.

When she thought she could stand the sweet agony no longer, he slipped two fingers inside her, beginning a fast pump. Within seconds violent shudders pulsed through her, sending her hips crashing against his wild thrusts and her mind falling into the yawning chasm of intense pleasure that was almost painful. As she spasmed, his mouth seared over her pussy, beautifully hot. He sucked her while his tongue continued to play with her clit, drawing out her orgasm.

By the time he was finished, she lay spent and drained on the sand.

Drained and wanting more.

She opened her eyes, and when he saw her watching him, he gazed away as if ashamed of what he'd just done.

But he *shouldn't* be ashamed. She loved the way his hot tongue seduced her clit. Loved the way his fingers thrust inside her. Most of all she loved the sparks of desire she'd seen brewing in his eyes when he gazed at her.

"Jacob, please come with me. Run with me. You need your freedom too," she whispered as desperation once again took hold.

She'd seen the cold, dead look in his eyes when he'd first come to her on the beach. He was dead inside, living a life he didn't want. She knew it even if he hadn't said it. Just being with her for a few minutes, he looked so alive. They needed to explore their feelings for each other and the only way they could do that was to spend time together.

His next words devastated her.

"I'm supposed to kill you, Hannah. I can't do that. But I can't let you go either or run away with you."

He wouldn't let her go?

Confusion and fear ripped through her, bringing a sting of tears to her eyes.

"Please, you have to let me go. Please, I'll do anything you want, Jacob. But I need my freedom."

His eyes snapped bright at her words.

"Anything?" he breathed.

"Whatever you want."

Her voice didn't give away the fact her insides quivered. She'd always wanted Jacob, but not like this.

"Let's go to my car," he instructed.

She hesitated. Whoever had called her on the communicator would be coming for her. She couldn't let them see Jacob or they would leave.

She held her breath as he gazed down between her spread legs. Strangely enough, she didn't feel the least bit ashamed.

Why should she?

Deep in her heart she knew Jacob Romero was a good man. At least that's what the other Slaves had always said. That's what she'd felt in her heart. She could only hope he still had some compassion left inside after years of killing people like her. Maybe she could change his mind? All she needed was a bit of time with him.

"I want a bed and twenty-four hours," he whispered.

Oh my goodness! He was taking her up on her offer!

If she thought her limbs were shaking before, they were spastic now.

Twenty-four hours? But what about her rescue boat to the Free States? Anxiety raged inside her. If she didn't go with him, her would-be rescuer would see him. Would know this place was compromised and never come back here for her. Another thought frightened her even more. If Jacob found out this was a contact spot for the Underground Railway he'd capture her would-be rescuers. It would ruin the chances for others coming after her.

Her blood froze as another thought formed. Unless he already knew this was a rendezvous point.

"How'd you find me?"

She had to know the answer. Had to know if this place was compromised.

"Lara told me."

Hannah felt as if a sledgehammer slammed into her stomach. If she hadn't been lying down she would surely have fallen from the betrayal shifting through her like raw fire.

"Why would she tell you I was here? How did she know? I didn't tell her."

"She didn't know for sure. She said a Slave mentioned this place while she lay dying. That maybe you thought it was a contact point for the Underground Railroad. It isn't a contact point, Hannah. If it was, you wouldn't still be here."

But they had called her! *Lara, how could you betray me like this?*

"Don't be mad at her. I promised her I wouldn't hurt you," he said softly as if reading her mind. "I was desperate to find you. There are other Hitmen out there looking for you too. I'm not the only one. Simon has put a big bounty on your head. You're the only one of his..."

He hesitated a moment as if wondering what word he should call her.

"You're the only one who has been on the run for this long without capture," he said.

Hannah tried hard not to turn her head toward the ocean. Toward freedom.

Instead, she locked her gaze onto Jacob, who now studied her.

Sympathy raged in his eyes, and it truly seemed as if he believed this place had nothing to do with the Underground Railroad. She needed to get him away from here so he wouldn't know the truth.

Agreeing to sleep with him was the only way out. She had to do it. She had to trust he would let her go afterward. She would come back here and wait again. He might follow her, but the next time she would make sure he didn't see her.

"What's your answer, Hannah?" he whispered.

She wanted to ask him what he would do if she said no. She didn't ask. She would use this opportunity to draw him away from here. To save the place for others. And for herself.

She could try and change his mind and get him to come with her and she could make sure her heart knew the truth about him too and that he wasn't just a fantasy man.

Reluctantly Hannah nodded.

Jacob hoisted himself off her and then kneeled between her legs. To her surprise, he reached down and his long fingers intertwined with her own.

"Your twenty-four hours start when we get to a motel."

Inwardly, she shivered. His words and his warm touch screamed pleasure as he helped her to her feet. She suddenly realized her dream of sleeping with Jacob was about to come true. She just hadn't figured it would be this way.

Chapter Two

HE WAS INSANE. TOTALLY crazy.

Or maybe he was in love?

No, not love. Lust.

He was lusting after a woman he had no business lusting after. She was a Breeding Slave. A runner.

He was a Hitman. A killer.

They were from two different worlds.

But that hadn't prevented him from being friendly with her at his uncle's breeding plantation. It hadn't prevented him from being sexually attracted to her or from wanting to claim her for his very own.

And she'd been the only woman he'd really wanted to fuck. The only one who was totally off-limits.

One beautiful black-haired five-foot-nine-inch Breeding Slave had gotten under his skin the minute he'd seen her step out of his uncle's vehicle that sparkling August afternoon four years ago. It was her seductive-as-sin curvy body that first captured his attention. Long, luscious legs were what he noticed next.

The rest of her was just as good. She had a creamy complexion, a heart-shaped face, perfectly arched eyebrows, a nice nose, red pouty lips and the most intoxicatingly exotic slanted green eyes. But all Breeding Slaves were genetically designed for perfection. To be physically eye-pleasing to the couples who wanted them to bear their children. So he shouldn't have really been surprised by his reaction.

However, there was something different about Hannah. Something deeper than her looks. He didn't know what exactly. Perhaps instinct that she was *the one*. Maybe the tenderness he saw in her eyes when she'd looked at him that day when they'd been introduced.

Or it could have been her scent. The minute she'd come close to him he'd noticed her freshness. Pure and innocent and oh-so-sweet.

For months on end after first seeing her he'd masturbated like crazy just thinking about her.

He'd been visiting his uncle's plantation at the time. His uncle always thought Jacob came to see him, but the truth was he liked to visit the Breeding Slaves and Studs he'd grown up with when he'd spent carefree summers there with his brothers. The slaves were nice people. Friendly, down-to-earth folks. Not false and bitter like most of the humans he dealt with in the city.

Truth was, he was fond of the women slaves, and when one or several suggested they have sex for old times' sake or for him to let off some steam, he willingly obliged. No red-blooded man could resist such sexy offerings. The fact they still wanted to be friends with him, even after knowing he killed their kind, and that they still wanted sex with him, seemed to make his life a bit more tolerable.

He'd had many a sleepless night over killing runaways. Most of his hits died instantly, not knowing a death laser with their name on it was mere feet away. He preferred not to give them a warning. Preferred not to see the fear in their eyes when they saw him.

Sometimes though, they sensed he was there and turned around to face their death head-on. It was harder to push the firing button when he saw the dreams in their eyes. But it was what he was drafted and trained to do. Kill or be killed. That was the motto for the Hit Association. A Hitman who didn't get his target would become one himself.

Every year that passed, his job became harder. He wanted to let those people go. Wanted to become a target himself. And then it would all be over.

But his guilt and suicidal thoughts grew dimmer when he'd seen Hannah that very first time. The iciness hardening his numb heart melted just a bit more. She was the most beautiful young woman he'd ever seen. And every time he saw her since that first time, the ice inside him thawed just a little bit more. Just as it had today on the beach.

When his uncle's message came, informing him of Hannah's Breeding Ceremony, giving Jacob his blessing to fuck her, it had been all too bittersweet. His uncle had given the same blessing to all his brothers.

When he'd come to his uncle's plantation, Hannah was gone.

Escaped.

A goddamn runner.

And he was in trouble.

One taste of her and he was hooked. She tasted better than he ever imagined.

All sweet and cinnamony. And the musical cries of her aroused whimpers as she climaxed... Jacob couldn't help but groan inwardly as he remembered the way her hips thrust her drenched pussy into his face, encouraging him to sip more of her heavenly juices.

She was one hell of a sexy woman. Even now as she sat beside him in the passenger side of his vehicle, stiff as a corpse, he could feel the sexual energy pouring out of her and over him.

Her full breasts heaved seductively with her every inhalation. Her lush mouth was set in grim determination.

She would do anything he wanted, she'd said.

And he accepted her offer.

Oh man. What had he done?

He couldn't even look at himself in the rearview mirror. If he did, he'd see the truth flashing in his eyes.

Breeding Slave or not, Hannah was *his* woman.

And now he had her.

Instead of feeling happy, he felt anxious.

She should be dead now. Dead on the beach.

She wasn't. Simply because he hadn't had the heart to do his job. Instead of doing his job, he'd walked down to the beach with full intention of warning her of the danger she was in by staying at the deserted mansion. That if her friend Lara knew about this place, someone else would know too and they'd come gunning for her to collect the huge bounty on her head.

But the closer he came to her, the more he wanted to taste her.

To make love to her.

Frig!

The Hit Association would kill him when they found out what he'd done. And what he was about to do.

Strangely enough, he didn't care what they did to him. Not anymore. He had Hannah and he was taking her to God only knew where.

When he first spotted her this morning, hiding in the deserted mansion, he should have simply walked away. Let someone else do the kill job. But he didn't want her dead. He just wanted her.

Lying on top of her on the beach after he'd tackled her had sealed his fate and hers as well.

He needed to make love to her. Needed to taste every part of her body. Needed to sink his aching cock deep into her.

He wanted to feel again. To feel like a man. To forget he was a killing machine.

He should apologize for frightening her.

But he wouldn't do it. Couldn't.

At least not yet.

He needed her to be afraid of him. It would keep her in line.

"I think I'm going to be sick." Her soft voice broke into his thoughts.

He wasn't surprised. The sharp curves along the coastal highway just about made him heave his guts too. Or maybe she was sick because she was so afraid of him. Man, he should have turned the laser gun on himself and blasted his head off. Then he would never have scared her.

"I'll pull over."

She nodded numbly, her hand clamped over her luscious mouth.

He whipped the car off the deserted two-lane highway and onto a dirt road lined with pine trees. A moment later they entered a small clearing.

She pushed the door open even before the car rolled to a stop.

He grimaced as she bent over and wretched. The sound was hollow and ugly.

A memory zipped through his brain. A memory of the slaves' retching when they'd become pregnant. He shouldn't think about it. He should shove those memories right out of his mind. Pretend they were nightmares, not reality.

What he needed was a good stiff drink. Needed to get himself stone-cold drunk and forget everything.

On suddenly shaky legs he climbed out of the car and inhaled the fresh pine-scented air.

Lifting his head, he winced at the intense confusion brewing in Hannah's eyes. She wiped the back of her hand across her mouth and watched him warily.

"Are you okay?" he asked.

Her eyes widened in disbelief and then an angry red blush whipped across her cheeks.

"I told you, I'll do anything you want. But I have to hear you say you'll let me go after we have sex. I need to believe I can trust your word. That you are an honorable man."

Honorable man? If he was so honorable he'd be telling her the truth. That he hadn't been able to stop thinking about her since the first day he'd seen her. That he'd stayed away from her because he didn't want to lose his heart and soul to her if he so much as touched her.

And he had been right to stay away.

The desperation in her eyes forced him to lie. "I give you my word."

"Then take me. Now. We can do it in the backseat."

He felt his jaw open in surprise.

Felt the guilt at wanting to fuck her take over. He could still taste the sweetness of her juices in his mouth. Oh, he wanted her. Wanted her so much he didn't think his entire body and mind had ever hurt so bad for a woman.

Pressing a button on the electronic card that he kept on a secured chain on his belt, he watched the trunk of his car pop open. Strolling to the trunk he opened the lid of the two-foot-by-two-foot black cooler that all squad vehicles were outfitted with. Being a Hitman had its benefits.

His car had state-of-the-art equipment. Satellite radio, global tracking systems, laser-proof windows and dent-proof plastic chassis, not to mention self-sealing and self-inflating tires if some sharp object punctured through the plastic-belted rubber.

All the food and drinks were free too when he showed his identification, so he was able to keep his cooler fully stocked. Accommodations and female entertainment were also free when he was out hunting down a hit.

For a split second he almost grabbed the antique bottle of tequila he kept in storage in the cooler. He could get drunk. He'd done it before on many occasions. It helped loosen him up.

But getting drunk wouldn't solve any problems this time around. Sure, he might forget them for a while, but after he came down, his troubles would still be here.

Beautiful, sexy Hannah would still be here.

Grabbing the neck of a cold blue metal bottle, he twisted off the silver tin lid and strolled toward Hannah with it.

"I won't touch you. Not if you don't want me to." He found himself saying as he offered her the sweet aqua drink.

Now it was her turn to be surprised. The fear in her eyes diminished, replaced by a sparkle of hope as she accepted the bottle.

"What are you saying? Are you letting me go?"

"No."

She bit her bottom lip and he saw the tears well in those gorgeous green eyes.

"Dammit! Don't cry," he snapped harshly.

"You've changed your mind, haven't you? You're going to kill me, aren't you?"

"I said I won't and I won't."

"What do you want from me?"

"I want to make love to you." The words escaped his mouth before he could stop them.

A frown burrowed between her dark eyebrows.

"You just said if I don't want to—"

"I don't want just sex. I want you," he said.

She blinked at him.

He cursed softly at the godawful confusion etching her face and reached into his back pocket for the item stashed there.

"Here. Chew on this when you finish the drink. It'll take the bile out of your mouth." He held out a wrapped stick of pine-mint gum. He used pine-mint gum after a drinking spree. Covered up the foulness of his breath.

She took it and lifted the bottle to her seductive mouth. God, what he wouldn't do to have her warm lips kissing his aching shaft. Sucking his hot flesh just as she was sucking on that bottle.

He shook the erotic thoughts away.

"I'm going to make a call," he instructed. "I'm keeping an eye on you, so stay right here."

She winced at his harsh tone and he cursed himself for being so gruff with her.

Keeping an eye on her, he made his way back to the car so she couldn't hear. From the pouch on his belt he unsecured his communicator.

He needed to stall for time. Needed to figure out what the hell he should do with Hannah.

After instructing the communicator which number he wanted, he listened anxiously to the beeps on the other end. His uncle's secretary answered and put Jacob straight through to Simon.

"Jacob! How the hell are you? I know you have good news for me."

"Cut the pleasantries, Uncle Simon."

His uncle's voice immediately sobered. "Is she dead?"

"She ran when she saw me." At least that wasn't a lie.

He cursed a long line of blue words that made Jacob wince.

"I thought they taught you better in that damn hit school, boy!"

"I'm in hot pursuit," he reassured.

Jacob watched Hannah as she leaned over and used her fingertips to comb out the tangles in her long brown hair. Man, what he wouldn't do to be able to thrust his fingers through those silky strands. To feel their softness flood his palms.

"Did you hear what I said?" his uncle snarled.

"What?"

"I said it's urgent she's removed. I want you to bring me back her head."

"I hear you. It'll be done." The mere thought of hurting her more than he'd already done made sour bile bite the back of his throat.

"I want her dead. She's humiliated me by running. It's a slap to our reputation as men when a Breeder Slave doesn't want to be fucked by a Romero. Just kill her! You know what'll happen to you if you don't."

There it was. The warning.

Get the hit. Or get hit. The Hitman's code stating a Hitman would die if he ever gave up on getting a hit.

"I'll call when the job is done," Jacob said between clenched teeth. He disconnected the call. Speaking with his uncle would hopefully buy him some time. Would make him think his nephew was doing his job. Another thought hit him and he quickly instructed the communicator to dial a different number.

He sighed in relief when a familiar man's voice answered on the first ring.

"I'm in deep shit, Tool. Really deep shit," Jacob blurted.

The man on the other line chuckled. "What else is new? What happened this time? You smash up the company car again? They short-change your paycheck?"

Jacob drew in a deep breath and almost revealed his problem. Almost confessed he had his hit right here and he wasn't going to kill her.

Deep in his heart he sensed he could trust Tool with the truth. But he just couldn't take the chance. It was better that he trusted no one. Not even his best friend, who, unfortunately, was also a Hitman. Thankfully though, Tool had been recently injured and was on office duty while recuperating. He would have access to areas Jacob didn't. Tool could buy him time.

"My hit saw me. She ran."

"You're losing your touch, bud. So, what do you need?"

"I need twenty-four hours of down time so I can relax. I can't do my job if I'm wound up. That's why she got away. I need no interruptions whatsoever. I've found a willing woman and we need some privacy. When I'm relaxed, I'll go after the hit," he lied.

"Holy Armageddon, my man! It's about time! Haven't I told you fucking a willing woman is the only way to relax? Christ, you Breeding-Slave-loving boys are so damn stubborn. You guys just don't listen to me. The fucking is much sweeter when you work for it. What is it that you need?"

"I need you to turn off the tracker in my car."

"What?"

"You heard me."

Tool's tone turned wary. "You know I'm not supposed to do that."

"Can you do it anyway? Divert my whereabouts. Keep it between us?"

"Must be some woman."

"She is. She's married and doesn't want to take the chance of being identified," he lied.

Silence on the other end. He could almost hear Tool's mind grinding with curiosity. Jacob and a married woman? That would be a first.

A moment later his friend's curse of defeat wafted over the line.

"I don't like this."

"Thanks, Tool."

"Twenty-four hours?"

"Twenty-four hours."

"Consider it done. I'll call you when your time's up," Tool said, and disconnected.

Jacob stuffed his communicator back into the pouch.

When he turned around, he froze.

Hannah stood right there. Not more than two feet from him.

Uncertainty filled her green eyes. A wobbly smile was plastered on her rosy lips.

His gaze lowered. His eyes widened.

Oh boy. This could not be happening. And yet it was.

She stood before him.

A goddess.

A very naked goddess.

His greedy gaze raked over her voluptuous figure. Although she was a Copy, he knew she'd been genetically engineered to not only be attractive to potential couples who wanted her as their baby's supplier, but also so she could produce attractive offspring, as well as to be pleasing to the male eye so the Studs selected to breed her would find her irresistible.

She had a waist that curved inward, hips and breasts that curved outward, giving her body an hourglass look. Hungrily, he scanned her shapely legs to the nude mons hiding her plump clit and tight vagina from his view.

His shaft sprang to life. Heated like molten steel. Hardened into an iron bar.

He remembered the delicate taste of her. The soft, hot feel of her pulsing clit against his mouth as he'd drained the sweetness from her cavern.

Mouth suddenly dry, he swept his gaze over her slightly rounded abdomen to her cute little belly button, her satiny belly and finally up.

To his disappointment her silky hair hid those full breasts from his view.

Jacob let out a ragged breath.

He should tell her to cover herself. Should tell her to run. To get away from him.

But he could say nothing. He could do nothing. Do nothing but stand there and hover at this dangerous line between wanting her and doing what was right by her.

"Jacob?" she said softly.

"Don't do this, Hannah..."

He cursed beneath his breath as she took a step forward.

What the hell was she doing? He'd already told her she didn't have to have sex with him.

She took another step closer.

He took one step back.

The wobbly smile on her pretty face turned into one of curiosity as she tilted up one corner of her lip. A dimple sparkled in her left cheek. Fuck! He loved that dimple.

Her eyes were hot with blatant desire as her gaze slid over his face. Before he knew it she stood right there in front of him. Barely a foot apart.

He breathed in her scent. She smelled fresh and salty like the ocean. A hint of the pine-mint gum she'd been chewing wafted into his nostrils.

Desire rumbled through him. He needed to touch her. Needed to show her he'd never hurt her.

With trembling hands, he reached out.

She inhaled softly as he parted the veil of her silky hair to reveal swollen breasts with plump pink nipples.

His legs watered. His self-control wavered.

He forced himself to close his eyes in an effort to gather the strength he needed to keep himself from touching her.

"Don't look away," she breathed.

Her hand came up and she cupped his chin. The gentle touch of her warm fingers against his skin made him groan.

Her body heat cradled him. Made him wish she was his forever.

He trembled as her other hand dipped inside his pants. Her fingers splayed flat against his belly. Only inches from his rock-hard cock. He felt his erection growing in anticipation.

"You don't have to do this, Hannah," he croaked.

"Yes, I do."

"Why?"

"Because...I want to. I've wanted to for a long time."

Oh man!

Her electric fingers slid around his hard shaft. Her hot touch made him harden violently. Made his sensitive flesh ache with a raging heat. A need that shattered his self-control.

Roughly he grabbed her by her bare shoulders. The silkiness of her velvety skin seared against his fingertips. Her warm pine-scented breath cascaded against his cheeks. Drowned his senses.

Her hand urged his chin toward her luscious, trembling lips.

This couldn't be happening. This had to be another dark fantasy. Another fantasy in an endless string of them.

"Hannah?"

"Shhhh." Her breath washed warm and minty against his face.

Oh boy, this was real.

The impact of her soft mouth upon his lips devastated him. It hurled him into another world. A world of pleasure so intense he had to harden his hold on her shoulders or surely he would fall to his knees.

Her hand uncupped his chin as she deepened the kiss. His world tilted awkwardly. His breath caught in his lungs. His mouth opened wider, allowing her sweet tongue to enter.

She kissed him greedily, her burning mouth demanding. Her fierce strokes clashed with his tongue, creating such a wrenching desire deep in his soul he literally felt the coldness encasing his heart crack wide open letting in the warmth he'd craved so much.

Her other hand slid under his shirt and over the tight muscles of his chest. He inhaled sharply as she tweaked his sensitive nipples. Ripples of longing sent heated blood roaring to parts south. His shaft throbbed and a wild fever set through the rest of his body.

A guttural moan started somewhere deep in his chest and somehow became lost in his throat as her fingers slid sweetly along the length of his hard shaft.

Have mercy! He'd never been stroked with such tenderness before. Oh he wanted to be inside her. Wanted to feel her velvety muscles clamp around him as she welcomed him deep inside her.

When her hand left his nipple and headed toward the area beneath his arm, the area where he kept his weapon holstered, a wiggle of warning whispered in his ear.

Bitch. He should have known. He should have known she was only distracting him!

Before her hand could curl around his gun, he forced himself to rip his mouth free from her tormenting sweetness. A tiny cry of protest escaped through her slightly parted lips. The hot look in her eyes flared with disappointment.

"You're good, Hannah. Real good."

"What's wrong? I thought—"

"You thought you could keep me amused so you could go for my gun and I was stupid enough to fall for it."

A brief look of shame flittered across her face. A look that didn't set right with her natural beauty.

For a split second he believed she had wanted him to fuck her. But that would only be wishful thinking.

She looked away, her face flaming pink with embarrassment.

Dammit!

He should take her. Lean her over the hood of the car and just slide his cock into her. Right here. Right now. Take her hard and fast.

It sure as hell would ease the ache in his hard shaft. Yet he couldn't do it. Couldn't take advantage of her like this.

"Get dressed," he ordered.

At the sound of the harshness in his voice, he felt better. Felt more in control.

She moved away from him, but not before he saw the tears glisten in her eyes.

"Hannah!"

She stopped.

"Don't do that again. Not unless you really mean it. Next time I won't stop. Next time I'll fuck you so hard you'll be begging me to never stop."

He didn't miss the tremor zip through her body. Was she scared of his warning? Or had that been a shiver of excitement?

He watched her dress. Her movements graceful. Seductive. Damn arousing.

The thought of going into the woods and jerking himself off entered his mind. But he didn't. He couldn't afford to be out of her sight for too long.

When she was dressed, he grabbed her by the arm and hauled her to the other side of the car where the passenger door stood open.

"Get in the car, Hannah."

"You've changed, Jacob. You used to be kind and gentle. Now you're just a cold bastard."

Before he could say anything she broke free from his grasp, slumped into the car and slammed the door shut with such a force it hurt his ears.

She kept silent as he started the car and drove out of the secluded area onto the main road.

It was going to be the silent treatment, was it?

He could easily break that silence. He'd have her screaming with pleasure before too long. Then maybe when he had her out of his system, he'd finally be able to let her go.

Chapter Three

HANNAH JOLTED AWAKE. For a minute she had no idea where she was.

The feeling wasn't uncommon. Not with the way she'd been on the run the past few weeks. Despite having access to the abandoned stone mansion and the bed in the attic, she had slept there only a few times after arriving, preferring to sleep in a new place every few nights to avoid detection and mostly so she could watch the stars before she fell asleep. The taste of freedom had done that to her. Made her want to be outdoors as much as possible.

Now as she peered out the side car window, she blinked at the semidarkness of twilight enveloping the fast-moving landscape of rolling hills and tried to remember what had happened.

A split second later it all came crashing around her like a horrible landslide.

Jacob had captured her! Jacob the Hitman.

A seemingly cold bastard with dead eyes on the outside when she'd first whirled around to see him. Yet when he captured her and his body covered hers on the beach, something wild and lusty had been unleashed inside her. When his hot tongue scooped against her clit as he devoured her, she'd melted like liquid silver, her body betraying her with a power she couldn't ignore.

Hannah shivered involuntarily as she remembered pursuing him in the meadow. She'd been sick to her tummy due to the combination of the sharp turns on the road and the fear of being captured. When she'd watched him speaking on his communicator, his voice low and hushed, her imagination had gone crazy.

What was he saying? Who was he talking to? Was he telling his superiors he'd caught her? Had he lied to her? Would he kill her?

She'd been desperate once again to escape. Hadn't been thinking clearly.

The thought of being so close to freedom down at the beach and having it slip through her fingers had screwed her common sense.

She'd wanted him to fuck her in the meadow. So he would let her go. Not because she'd wanted it. But when she approached him in the meadow, he'd backed away from her, fear shining in his eyes. Fear and confusion.

Why was he scared of her? Why would he agree to the proposition of her allowing him to do whatever he wanted and then just change his mind?

If he was afraid of her, why should she be afraid of him?

Much-needed confidence flooded her, giving her the idea to go after his gun. And the only way to do that was to distract him with a kiss. When she'd kissed him, his searing warmth had curled through her body, pushing aside any remaining fear.

And when he'd returned her kiss...it was as if an electrical field encompassed them. A wild energy that zapped through her entire being, awakening all her senses into full alert.

His thick arousal had pressed intimately against her suddenly wet and eager pussy.

Oh sweet Armageddon! Suddenly she'd wanted him to bury his hot flesh deep inside her. To make her forget all her troubles. To make her remember why she'd fantasized about him over the years.

But when he broke the kiss and accused her of trying to steal his gun, she'd been stunned. Unable to comprehend why lust had overwhelmed her so much for a man who'd been sent to kill her. For a few beautiful seconds she'd forgotten why she'd come on to him, his kiss was so distracting.

But she'd recovered. Barely. Realizing getting his gun was the only way to escape. But what would happen when she had the weapon? She had no idea how to use one.

"There's a motel up ahead. There's a restaurant too if you're hungry." His voice snapped through her racing thoughts.

"I'm not hungry."

He said nothing as he took the exit.

A shiver ripped through Hannah as she watched him. His full mouth pouted. His handsome face, determined.

Had he changed his mind? Was he going to tell her the deal was still on? He'd said the deal would start when they reached the motel. Is that why he hadn't wanted to have sex with her in the meadow?

Her stomach tightened with dread.

Or was it anticipation?

Christ, she wasn't horny.

Just scared shitless. And desperate.

But if she was scared, why was she anxious to feel his warm lips sliding against hers again? Why did she want to feel his silk-encased cock throbbing in her hand again? And why was she hoping he would bring back those feelings of pleasure?

Maybe her thoughts were so focused on sex because she was distracting herself from thinking about the gun he'd been pointing at her on the beach? At the moment, when she'd seen the dead look in his eyes, would he have pulled the trigger if she hadn't run?

He pulled into the parking lot, jolting her from her thoughts.

The motel was a small one-story building. A bit run down, small and quaint, surrounded by a large meadow at the sides and a string of tiny pine trees along the front lawn.

He turned to her. "I'll go inside and register. The doors will be locked in here so don't try to leave. Don't worry about anyone seeing you, the windows are tinted. Are you sure you don't want anything to eat? I can pick something up. You can eat in the room."

Hannah shook her head.

Despite her stomach feeling settled, she was afraid she might puke again if she ate anything right now. He climbed out of the car, slammed the door shut and strolled toward the main entrance.

He looked tired, she thought as she watched him. He was a big, tall man dressed in traditional green Hitman garb. He was a very imposing figure who wore loose-fitting pants that did little to hide the provocative bulge between his thighs. He looked powerful. Sexy. Yet so dangerous.

The instant he disappeared into the building she tried to unlock the front doors and her stomach sank. Even the glove compartment was locked. She scanned the sterile, dark interior of the vehicle for any sort of weapon, knowing even if she found one she probably wouldn't be able to use it on him. He hadn't hurt her. Just frightened her so badly and pleasured her so nicely.

Hannah swallowed as she remembered yet again how big and silky his cock felt in her hands. He was so well hung, confirming what the Breeder Slaves had told her.

The thought of Jacob being with women made something, a bad feeling she didn't much like, roll through her.

She jumped when the door suddenly opened.

"Easy, it's just me. Come one, let's move fast. The coast is clear," he said, and held out his hand to her. It was a big hand, containing long, slender fingers that must have killed many people like her. Her heart thumped a mile a minute as her fingers curled around his so intimately she couldn't believe he would ever hurt her. Or anyone for that matter.

She forced herself to inhale slowly. To stay calm.

He wouldn't hurt her. She had to believe that. He'd always been kind to her in the past. Had always been friendly.

And she'd always wanted him.

Excitement mingled with dread as she stepped out of the vehicle.

It was dark now. Aside from another vehicle in the parking lot, the place looked deserted.

He could do whatever he wanted to do to her in the motel room and he still might not let her go.

Oh! She had to stop distrusting him or she'd go mad for sure.

He slammed the door, let go of her hand then took hold of her elbow. To her surprise, he held out a roll of antacids. He must have picked it up inside.

"For your stomach."

He was concerned for her health? Confusion gripped her gut and she accepted the roll.

"Room thirteen. To the left and on the end," he said as he walked beside her.

The urge to bolt was great. So great she almost ran. But the hold on her elbow was so gentle she once again knew he wouldn't hurt her. If she ran, he'd catch her in a split second.

He'd be angry. She didn't want him to be angry. She wanted to see life spring back into his eyes. To see happiness and love.

Oh Armegeddon! She was losing her mind! She felt as if she were on a wild bungee swing ride. The same kind she and her friends used to play with on the farm where she'd grown up.

All she had to do was place her feet into the loop at the end of the twelve-foot band that hung from the tree. Up and down she'd go.

Back then the odd queasy sensations had been so much fun. Now they weren't. One minute she knew she was safe with him and the next doubts flared through her like an explosion. Up and down.

Oh God, please help me to stay calm.

He pressed the red button on the tiny two-inch-by-two-inch white box he held in his hand. The door to room thirteen swung inward and Hannah stepped inside.

"Cozy little room," he said from behind her after flicking on the lights.

"Perfect." She managed a weak smile as she spied the double bed in the middle of the room. A pretty dark green comforter covered it. Fuchsia pillows along with the same color of sheets peeked out along the top edge of the comforter. On the wall above the bed hung a giant heart-shaped picture frame depicting a man and a woman holding hands as they walked through a dandelion-strewn meadow.

Freedom screamed out of the picture and Hannah found herself tensing with anxiety again.

If Jacob hadn't come when he had, she'd be on the boat to freedom now.

Yet if he hadn't come, she would never have seen him again.

Sadness tugged at her heart. Suddenly she wasn't sure if she was feeling sad because of the thought at never seeing Jacob again or from losing her freedom.

"You sure you're not hungry?"

"Food is the last thing on my mind," Hannah replied.

He scowled.

He'd been frowning since he finished going down on her on the beach. Was he sorry for pleasuring her? Or was it because he didn't know if he should let her go?

Hannah inhaled softly as she remembered the stories the older Breeder Slaves had told her about him. Before he'd left to be a Hitman, he'd always had a smile on his face. After he'd been drafted, he'd truly never smiled again. She wanted to see him smile.

Her heart wrenched at the self-conscious way he thrust his hand through his silky brown hair as he stood beside her, unsure of what to do next.

"If you have to go to the bathroom, go now. Leave the door open."

"So you can watch? I don't think so."

"Leave the door open or don't go. I won't watch."

"I don't have to go."

"Lie down on the bed then."

"What?"

"Lie down."

Oh God, he was going to start having sex with her now.

Shakily, Hannah went over to the side of the bed closest to the bathroom and sat on the lumpy mattress.

"Turn on the light on my side of the bed," he instructed.

Scooting across the bed, she turned on the light. He flicked the main ones off, throwing the room into semidarkness. Then he strolled to the bed like a lusty predator eying the mate he wanted. Her.

He watched her as she moved quickly back to her side, and then he crawled onto the bed beside her.

He was a big man and the bed springs creaked as he lay down fully clothed. Despite her nervousness, she noted he smelled kind of sexy in a rugged sort of way. He didn't even take off his black boots, but he did remove a black box, which she assumed was the tazer, a stun gun that paralyzed anyone it hit, from a holster on the outside of his boot. The laser gun quickly followed as he pulled it from his shoulder holster and placed it and the tazer within easy reach on the small stand beside the bed.

When he turned and saw her watching him, he frowned and then looked away and up to the ceiling.

"Just relax, Hannah. You're safe. For now."

For now?

Hannah's heart once again began to pound with anxiety.

"What's that supposed to mean?"

He ignored her question. "Give me your hand."

"What?"

"Either give me your hand or I'll have to slap on the cuffs."

Damn him! Why didn't he just get this over with and quit stalling? Reluctantly she held out her hand and he laced his fingers intimately with hers, holding her tight.

The warmth from his calloused hand sank deep into her flesh, branding her. Making her come alive with sensations that fired her blood.

He reached out and flicked off the lamp on the night table. The room plunged into darkness.

Immediately his scent swarmed all over her, resurrecting the memories of today. Making her remember how she'd touched him in the meadow. The crisp feel of his chest hairs beneath her fingertips as she'd pinched his pebble-hard nipples. The hot satiny feel of his skin and the underlying rigid stomach muscles quivering as she'd moved toward his cock.

His sexy scent had been her aphrodisiac, urging her on. The electricity springing up through her body as she'd touched his skin had made her fingers boldly wrap around the hot flesh of his thick penis.

The power throbbing against her fingers had been awesome. Heat had flooded throughout her. Thick and hot. Most of it settling low in her belly. Leaving her body and her senses blazing with uncontrollable want.

She'd wanted his hot body pinning her against the cold metal of his car. Wanted to feel the thick power of his fiery erection deep inside her as he slammed into her pussy in a desperate effort to put out the ache he'd created between her legs.

"Why did you run from the plantation, Hannah?" His rough voice broke her from her thoughts.

She blinked wildly into the darkness. The unexpected question stunned her. It made her remember the last night she'd been with Simon. Made her remember the helplessness enveloping her when he told her she was going to her Breeding Ceremony the next morning. Desperation had flooded her at the thought of so many men being set loose upon her.

She remembered the complaints from those Breeding Slaves who'd gone through their own Ceremony with more than one man. How tired and sore they'd been trying to accommodate their various sexual appetites. How happy they'd been to learn they were finally pregnant and would have some months of peace and quiet. But after the baby was born, it would start all over again with a Stud selected by a couple who wanted their own baby.

"I don't want to be a Breeding Slave," she blurted.

"You were created for that purpose. Conditioned for it. My uncle purchased you for that reason. You're his property. He can do with you what he pleases. The law is on his side."

She couldn't believe the coldness in his voice. The finality of his words.

"No man owns me," she snapped, feeling the raw anger rage through her.

She flinched as his fingers tightened around hers.

"Who the hell taught you this crap?"

"No one taught me. It's something I feel inside me. It's something I feel every time I watch a slave give birth to a baby. It rips out my heart to see her bond with her unborn child and then she is forced to give her baby away to strangers without being allowed to even hold it. I see the pain in their eyes. I feel their emotions as if they are my own. Being created to be a Breeder Slave isn't right. And there are the questions that haunt us too.

"How will the couple treat the baby? Will the child have a good life? Will he or she ever know where they truly came from? I don't want to go through that pain. I want one man for my children. Despite my conditioning, I know in my heart and my mind that I don't have to go through hell just because some man bought me. When an opportunity arose to try for freedom, I left."

Since learning of the Underground Railroad she'd had a couple of opportunities to escape, but she'd been too afraid of the unknown. Fortunately for her, she was more afraid of Judias.

Beside her, Jacob sighed heavily. "You've embarrassed the family. They're very upset. My uncle won't stop until I bring him your head as a trophy. Literally."

She shuddered at his words.

"I'm sorry for their pain. But I'm not sorry for following my heart." Aside from being Simon's anal sex toy over the years, he hadn't forced her to be with another man as he had with most of the other Breeder Slaves. She knew she was a part of his anal harem. He hadn't treated her badly. That is, until he decided it was time for her Ceremony. And his nephews had been kind to her too. Not taking advantage of their position over her as Simon had done.

Call it a forbidden dream for a Breeder Slave, but she wanted her freedom. Now more than ever.

Jacob didn't say anything, but his fingers loosened their grip ever so slightly around hers. Despite her best efforts to stop it, the intimate gesture calmed some of her anger.

"Go to sleep, Hannah. I'm very tired. I've barely slept for days while searching for you. We'll talk later," he said wearily.

Sleep? Was he serious?

He said nothing more, and when she heard his breathing soften a few moments later, she realized he'd already fallen asleep.

What in the world was going on with him? He said he'd barely slept for days. Insomnia? Or his need to be the first to get to her so he could save her?

No. Not save her. Fuck her. If he'd wanted to save her, he wouldn't have had his finger on the firing button of his laser gun on the beach when he'd come up behind her. Unless he'd changed his mind at the last moment, realizing he didn't want her dead?

Oh, she had to stop with these questions. Had to rest so she could be alert when the time came to escape. Reluctantly she closed her eyes.

Today's meadow adventure came swiftly to mind. She remembered the intimate way his erection pressed against the apex of her legs while she'd kissed him.

She'd never been sexually aggressive in her life. Not until today with Jacob.

Now that she'd crossed the line, she wasn't sure if she could stop herself from doing it again.

JACOB OPENED HIS EYES to find Hannah standing in the semidarkness beside the bed, looking down at him. Her hands cupped her naked breasts and she held them out to him in a blatant offer.

Carnal arousal speared through him at the sensual sight.

His breathing quickened. His cock hardened into a searing band of molten steel.

"What are you doing, Hannah?" he managed to croak.

"Giving us what we both want."

"You don't have to do this, Hannah. Not for me."

"I want you. I want your mouth all over me. I want you inside me."

She pressed her silky breasts closer to his face. They heaved gently with every breath. They tempted him as he'd never been tempted before.

His mouth watered as his gaze zeroed in on her large nipples.

Have mercy. How the hell could he resist such an offer?

He licked his lips in anticipation as she leaned closer. She moaned as he placed a teasing kiss at the tip of one plump nipple. It was a tight bud. A blossom of warmth. He smiled and drew the lush nipple into his mouth. Her flesh tasted like sweet nectar and sex.

His tongue teased the tight bud and she whimpered.

"Make love to me, Jacob. Fuck me hard."

"Oh my dear Hannah. I've wanted you for so long," he whispered around her nipple before sucking on it again.

She moaned again. It was an animalistic sound.

Too wild. Not at all what Hannah had sounded like when he seduced her pussy on the beach or when they'd kissed in the meadow.

A tinge of alarm zipped up his spine and he stopped suckling.

The moans continued.

What the hell?

Jacob opened his eyes and blinked at the harsh noises drifting through the darkness.

A dream?

Orienting himself, he quickly discovered the sounds weren't coming from Hannah but from the adjoining motel room.

Complements of the listening implants embedded into his ears when he became a Hitman, he was able to hear better than most humans and knew that to Hannah the sounds were probably faint. But he could hear everything as if they were right here in this room. Every squeak of the bed spring as the man thrust into the woman. Every gasp from her as she was impaled. The guttural groans as he worked harder toward his climax.

Jacob's cock pulsed at the erotic sounds. Pulsed and tightened into one hell of an aching rod.

He was about to pound on the wall to tell the lovers to quiet down when he realized Hannah was awake beside him. In the darkness he made out her curvy outline, complements of the heat-seeking infrared lens implanted into his eyes and wired to his brain. The lens was yet another feature Hitmen were given upon acceptance into the Hit Association. It allowed him to have night vision so he could hunt his prey in dark-lighting situations. Humans were automatically registered in his vision as red silhouettes.

And Hannah made one hell of a sexy-looking silhouette. She was lying on her back, her head turned toward him. Certain areas of her body—her lips, her breasts and nipples and a large area between her thighs were redder than other parts, signifying her arousal state. He could also feel how tight her warm fingers were wrapped around his as she listened to the lovers next door.

"I guess you hear the festivities," he whispered.

Her slight inhalation sounded so sexy he wanted to rip her clothes off and plunge himself deep inside her, making her cry out with desire. But he kept a tight control on himself. She didn't say anything for a long time as they both listened to the mating sounds from the couple.

Finally she spoke. "Why didn't you fuck me in the meadow or on the beach? Why did you tell your uncle you wanted to be the only one to fuck me during the Breeding Ceremony?" Her questions zeroed in on him like missiles.

"Go back to sleep, Hannah."

"Is that what you want? To have one child with me and then to let other men fuck me in the future? Simon seems to think after you've had me you wouldn't want me anymore."

Damn his uncle and damn her! He didn't want her to know how badly he wanted to have her as his own. But he was so tired. Tired of killing. Tired of living. Tired of wanting a woman he could never have.

"There are laws I have to uphold. I can't do what I want."

"You're doing it now."

"I'll pay for it in the end." With a laser blast to the head by another Hitman when he finally let her go. At least then she would be free and he would be dead. But he wanted to at least spend a little bit of time with her to see how things might have been between them.

"How will you pay?" she asked, and then he heard her gasp as realization dawned on her. It was common knowledge about the code of a Hitman. Common knowledge that sooner or later a Hitman would die at the hands of another. He'd killed several of them too when they'd let a target go.

Beside him, she shifted on the bed. With her lying on her side, he was able to make out her curvy hips and long legs. He could also feel her determination reach right out of the darkness and grab on to him. Could feel her sexy scent splash all around him.

"You would rather die than risk your life to be with me?" Disbelief etched her voice.

She was calling him a coward.

Bitch.

His heart pounded like a sledgehammer as the truth slapped him in the face. Acid churned his stomach. His cheeks twitched as he clamped his mouth shut and tried to temper his anger.

For weeks he'd been living on the edge, tensing every time his communicator crackled to life, informing him someone wanted to speak with him. He was that sure they would tell him Hannah had been killed. For weeks cold sweat clung to his body as he interrogated everyone at his uncle's plantation. The slaves had been surprised at his determination in getting answers. He'd been hard on them. Very hard.

Luck was on his side with Lara, Hannah's best friend. He'd interrogated her several times until she finally broke. Shame had filled him at the young Slave's frightened eyes as he'd threatened to beat her. Threatened to kill her and her unborn child if she didn't tell him where Hannah had gone. Of course, he would never have done that to Lara, but she didn't know that.

Shit. He had one bad temper when it came to Hannah's safety. Hadn't realized it until she'd run.

"And that's why so many of them escape from other plantations? That's why there's so many Hitmen and Hitwomen drafted and employed? Because the slaves enjoy their lot in life?"

He could hear the bitterness pouring out of her. Could see the red anger shifting through her body. He wasn't surprised.

Jacob's stomach heaved at the thought of all the people he'd killed in the name of duty. Killed simply because the government or their owners wanted them dead and the slaves wanted their freedom. And because he was a weak son of a bitch who couldn't go up against the Association and tell them he didn't want anything to do with being a Hitman. Hell, if he did that, he'd be dead too.

Instead, he'd just gone along with the hand dealt to him. Went along with his lot in life.

But Hannah had decided to fight against her intended fate. He envied her strength. He was too tired to be strong though. Too many years of feeling dead inside. Effectively feeling like a zombie.

Hell, he didn't deserve happiness in his life. Didn't deserve to have Hannah lying here on the bed beside him. He should have let her stay on the beach. He should have let her find her own way to freedom.

The moans from the couple next door grew frenzied, louder.

In response, Hannah tried to jerk her hand away from his grasp.

He wouldn't let her go and watched as more red areas sliced through her body. She was aroused and she was angry.

She sighed in frustration.

"I'm sorry about what happened today in the meadow," he whispered, trying to calm her.

"You could have taken me then. Why didn't you?"

"Because you don't want me," he admitted.

She remained silent for a long time after that. Secretly he hoped she would say she wanted him to make love to her here and now. She didn't.

"Yet you forced me to come with you, even when you knew I didn't want to have sex with you. Why?"

How the hell did he answer that one? Should he tell her the truth? Tell her he'd fallen in love with her the moment he'd seen her climb out of his uncle's vehicle after he'd brought her to the plantation?

"I haven't had sex with a woman in a long time," he admitted.

Oh heck, where had that come from?

"And I just happened to be the first woman you've come across who you've wanted to fuck in a long time?"

"Something like that."

She gave a strange little chuckle. "You're just like all the other men."

All the other men?

Anger erupted inside him. Anger at the thought of how close she'd come to being passed around to all his brothers and numerous other men.

"They see an attractive woman and they begin to fantasize. I know from the other Breeding Slaves some of the males can't even wait for the Ceremony before they force themselves on their selected mate."

"I know my uncle forced himself on you. I should have killed him before he took you."

He knew his uncle hadn't bred Hannah because he'd taken her as his own. Simon didn't like to share his women. He took them as virgins, and when he grew tired of them, he had them bred. Over the years, Jacob had fooled himself into thinking it was better she was with his uncle so she wouldn't be with other men. Had told himself Hannah wasn't his for the taking. He'd been wrong. He should have taken her all those times he visited the plantation. Taken her and told her she belonged to him and no other man. He'd been a damn idiot for admiring her from afar and not letting her know his feelings.

"Your uncle owned me, Jacob. I didn't have much choice in the matter of entertaining him. Submitting to a master's wishes is what we've been conditioned to do."

Strangely enough there was no bitterness in her voice. Okay, so he was a fucking coward. Hannah pegged him right. He should have done something about her. But what the fuck had he expected her to do?

She was a Copy. The sole purpose she'd been created for was to be a Breeding Slave not his wife.

Beside him, Hannah wiggled around again and a moment later her sweet breath cascaded over his face.

"I think you're one of those men who fantasize and don't do anything about it, Jacob. I think you've been fantasizing about me for a long time, haven't you?"

Jacob tensed at her question. "Be quiet and go to sleep, Hannah."

"I'll be quiet if you tell me the truth. Why are we here?"

"You're here because I want to keep you alive and I'm just too tired to think about how to do it right now. I love you more than my own life, Hannah. Now will you please just be quiet so I can get some sleep?"

Chapter Four

WITH HIS WORDS HE'D meant to shock her into silence. Just long enough so he could get a little bit of rest in order to think clearly. Obviously he wasn't thinking clearly at all and that's why Hannah was still alive and lying here beside him in a motel room.

He needed to put things into perspective. Needed to think of a way to get her to safety. And he could do it only by closing his fucking eyes and sleeping. Unfortunately his words didn't have the desired effect. She kept on talking as if he hadn't just spilled his guts to her.

"So you really aren't going to kill me?" she whispered, disbelief still etching her words.

Dammit! He'd just told her he loved her more than his own life and she still thought he would kill her. He'd really screwed up everything, hadn't he? Now she was not only afraid of him but she didn't trust him either.

"You have to ask?" he snapped a bit too harshly.

Guilt at his gruffness slammed into him. Despite his behavior, he could feel some of the tension ease from her. Could hear her breathing deepen with realization as his words finally sank in. And he could hear something else too. Something besides the exotic moans from the couple next door.

The implants allowed him to detect out-of-the-ordinary sounds like the quiet rattling noise that raised the fine hairs on the back of his neck. Obviously someone was trying to pry open their door. He swung his gaze in that direction and had no trouble making out the red silhouette, which indicated a human standing on the other side of the door.

A hot slice of betrayal slammed into his guts.

Son of a bitch!

His best friend Tool must have betrayed him and alerted the Association about his request in turning off the tracker on his vehicle. Obviously Tool had left the tracker on so someone could find Jacob. If they found Hannah here with him, they were both dead.

Trying hard to ignore the raging panic grabbing hold of his senses, Jacob slid out of bed and grabbed the two weapons he'd set on the table earlier.

"You need to go out the back window, get to my car and get the hell out of here," he whispered, knowing that if it was a Hitman on the other side of the door he or she most likely saw and heard the two of them. Even as he said it he realized how futile it would be for her to escape in his car with the tracker on it. If he couldn't hold off whoever was out there, and they got on to their communicator to request backup, she'd be surrounded in minutes.

Immediately she sat up in bed, her red silhouette tense.

"What's wrong?"

"Someone's found us."

Her sharp curse spiraled out of the darkness and she moved off the bed before he knew what was happening. A moment later he saw her silhouette as she peered out the back window.

He kept his voice low as he joined her and slapped the tazer into her palm.

"The weapon is loaded. Just press the green glow and you can do a lot of damage."

She started to speak when he pressed a finger to her lips and handed her the car card. He could only hope she understood that he wanted her to get out of here with the vehicle.

"If there's too many of them...make a run for it."

Although he knew she wouldn't make it if she chose to run, her death would be quick and virtually painless. And if she died, he died.

She tensed as he edged in closer to her. He stared at her luscious lips, wanting to kiss her goodbye. Her lips parted as if expecting he would do what they both wanted.

Instead he bent his head so his mouth was not even an inch from her ear. As he spoke, he swept his hands through the lush strands of her hair, hoping the whispering sounds would conceal what the intruder might hear.

"Ditch the car as soon as you can because there's a tracker on it. I'll try to hold them off as long as possible."

She didn't move. Her eyes pierced the darkness and in the blue glaze of moonlight he could see her studying him. Could feel her desperation sift through the air. It was as if she knew he most likely would be dead by morning if he didn't go with her.

"I'm not leaving without you," she suddenly said.

"I'm not arguing with you. Go. Now."

Gazing back at the door, he saw the red silhouette still standing there. He'd straightened, obviously giving up on the idea of a surprise visit. His arm was lifting as if to knock on the door. A second later the sharp sound snapped through the room.

"Come with me. Please," she whispered.

He shook his head and let go of her silky hair. If he could stall whoever was out there, Hannah just might have the slightest chance in getting away.

When she didn't move, impatience raged through him. Reaching around her, he pressed the unlock button. The window slowly opened outward. Poking his head out, he breathed a sigh of relief when he saw no splash of red indicating a human figure. Out back, the coast was clear.

The red silhouette still stood at the door.

"Open up, Romero!" came the shout. He recognized the voice.

He was a Hitman who went by the name Sawblade. He was one mean son of a bitch.

"Don't argue. Just go."

She didn't move and he saw the fear reflected in her eyes. The sight of her being afraid for him just about broke his heart. He wished he could give her a good-bye kiss but there just wasn't any time.

"Whatever happens, don't look back."

"Oh God," she whispered.

She hesitated just long enough to piss him off so he grabbed her by the waist and easily hoisted her to the windowsill, practically shoving her out the window.

Then he headed for the door.

EASING HER WAY ALONG the moonlit side of the building, Hannah's heart thundered in her ears as she stumbled through the tall weeds that lined a cracked sidewalk.

Because I love you more than my own life. Jacob's words rang through her head like a death chant.

How could he love her? They barely knew each other. Had seen each other several times over the years. Had spoken politely. She was the one who was in love with him, not the other way around.

Damn him! She was so confused.

She'd felt his fear by the way he'd practically shoved her out the window. Saw the terror in his eyes when he'd made sure she was out of the room before turning and heading for the door.

The fear and terror hadn't been for his life but for hers.

Because I love you more than my own life.

When he'd said those words moments earlier, she'd been literally stunned. The words hadn't really meant anything because she still suspected he would kill her. But then the realization slowly sunk in. He could have had sex with her whenever he'd wanted to. On the beach. In the meadow. Here in the room.

But he hadn't.

He'd gone down on her like a desperate man who thought he'd lost something valuable and suddenly found it again.

Hannah shook the thoughts away and peeked around to the front of the motel. Aside from the dim lamps shining onto the parking lot, she didn't see anyone.

Jacob could have saved himself a lot of trouble just by forcing himself on her and then killing her. Instead, he'd put his life on the line by bringing her here to a motel. In the meadow he said he wanted to be with her, but only if she wanted to be with him.

Sweet Armageddon! His words hadn't really meant anything because she'd been too afraid to allow them to register. Her freedom had been snatched away. She'd feared for her life and she'd been wallowing in self-pity that she hadn't really realized what he'd said.

He wanted her. He loved her. He was going to die here because of her.

Anger roared up through her, pushing away her fear.

Damn him!

She should forget about him. Get her ass in gear, get into his car and make her escape. He said the vehicle had a tracker. This she could use for her benefit by going in the opposite direction of where she really wanted. Instead of heading directly for the ocean, she could drive inland and ditch the vehicle then double back on foot. In a few days she could be back at the stone mansion and waiting for another chance at a rescue.

She also had a weapon to protect herself. This opened new possibilities.

Self-protection in the Free States. And maybe getting out of here alive was another one.

From their room location she could hear Jacob talking with the man.

"You know it's against policy to have them turn off the tracking devices, Romero." A gruff voice echoed from the open doorway of their room.

"Just wanted some time off to spend with a beautiful woman, Sawblade. I cleared it with Tool," came Jacob's casual reply.

"So where is this beautiful woman? Why have her sneak her out the back window?" the man named Sawblade asked.

"Because she doesn't want to be seen. Isn't that obvious? You leave and she'll come back and we'll continue where we left off."

Sawblade chuckled. "Or I can stay and we have a threesome."

Jacob answered, but his voice was muffled as the newcomer stepped into the room she'd left only moments ago.

Okay, now was the time to move!

Crouching, with tazer gun in one hand and the car card in the other, she ran the twenty feet to Jacob's vehicle. Inserting the card into the slot, she breathed a sigh of relief as the door clicked open.

She was about to get in when a man's shout slammed through the air. She didn't dare stop. She dropped into the driver's seat, slammed the door shut, locked it, slid the card into the ignition and the car purred to life.

Before she could put it into drive, white sparks exploded off the front window mere inches from her face, momentarily blinding her.

Hannah clamped down the urge to scream and slumped low in the bucket seat.

"Get the hell out of here, Hannah!" Jacob yelled as he began firing at the Hitman. Sawblade spun around, crouched and returned fire. Then he turned and began firing at her.

She screamed as an array of white laser rays sparked off the plastic windshield, leaving giant lashes of black crisscrossing over the damaged windows.

Dammit! She had to get out of here and fast.

Slamming her foot onto the accelerator, she felt herself lurch as the car ploughed backward a few feet before she quickly whipped the car into drive. In front of her, Jacob had taken cover behind the Hitman's parked car and both men were firing at each other.

Hannah's heart lodged in her throat when she spotted a dark patch on Jacob's upper left thigh.

Oh my God! He's been hit!

Panic edged her into making a swift decision. Turning the car into the parking spot beside Jacob, she flung open the passenger door.

"Go! Get the fuck out of—" Bursts cut off the rest of what he was saying and Hannah screamed as another array of white sparks zipped off one of the back side windows.

Jacob returned fire on Sawblade.

"Move!" she screamed at him, her gut twisting with anxiety when he popped off a couple more shots before gazing over at her again.

Realizing she was still here, he swore violently and snapped a few more laser shots in rapid fire. She heard Sawblade cry out and drop to the ground. He was still.

Thankfully Jacob dove in.

Within a split second she had the car in reverse yet again and flew out of the parking lot. Hannah screamed and Jacob cursed as a wild array of white sparks shrieked off the back window, leaving a crisscross of black lashes.

A quick glance into the rearview mirror showed the Hitman lying on his back, gun in hand, firing erratically as he watched them leave.

She watched as the Hitman struggled into a standing position.

"He's coming after us," she cried out.

Adrenalin roared through her.

The Hitman stumbled toward his car.

"He's coming!" she shrieked.

"He's not," Jacob said through deep gasps. His voice was way too casual under the circumstances.

Sickness clawed at her belly as she spied the Hitman place his hands on the trunk of his car to steady himself. Suddenly he let go of the trunk and dropped to his knees. He tried clawing at the bumper to keep himself erect but then in slow motion he crumpled to the pavement.

He was still.

"He's dead," Jacob whispered.

"How would you know? He may just be wounded," she said, flipping her eyes between the rearview mirror and the road ahead.

"I hit him in the heart. He was shooting and walking on sheer adrenaline. He won't be coming after us. But the rest of the Hit Association will be. Probably sooner rather than later. We need to ditch this vehicle and do it really soon."

"You mentioned a tracker. Is there any way I can disconnect it?"

"Not unless you have a bomb. The tracker is encased in a tamper-proof material. Many have tried to disconnect it and failed."

"How about your leg? Do you think you can walk on it?"

"Just slow the car down and I'll jump."

She swore and quickly flipped on the lock to his side of the vehicle, making sure he couldn't follow through on his threat.

Shit. Was the man suicidal or what?

He'd taken her to a motel instead of killing her. He'd killed a Hitman for her. Now he was threatening to jump out of the vehicle so she could escape more easily.

"I'll stop a few miles up ahead and check on your wound. Then we'll decide what to do."

He didn't say anything for a few minutes but she could hear his ragged, barely controlled breathing rip through the interior of the vehicle.

"We need to ditch the car," he said again after a few minutes. His voice sounded weaker. Desperation cleaved through her.

"I know where we can hide." Even as the words tumbled out of her mouth she didn't know if she should risk taking Jacob there.

He closed his eyes and his next words gave her the oddest thrill.

"Don't think that just because you saved my life you're off the hook, Hannah. I will take you. When the time is right, I will make love to you as a man makes love to his woman."

His woman. Not his uncle's Breeding Slave. Not a Copy. But a woman. Oh sweet heavens!

She tried to grab hold of her senses, but her mind was fragmenting at the thought of Jacob making love to her. Fragmenting into lush visions of his naked body covering hers. Taking her. Claiming her.

"I told you I belong to no man." Her whispered words didn't ring true even to her own ears.

"You will be mine, Hannah. In every way possible. That's a promise."

The confidence in his voice left little doubt he would follow through with his promise.

Suddenly she couldn't wait for his pledge to come true.

JACOB DRIFTED OFF. He hadn't wanted to but the burning pain in his thigh was so bad he'd forced himself into unconsciousness. And with the unconsciousness came the erotic dreams of Hannah.

Her silky vagina wrapped tight around the length of his swollen cock as he plunged into her. She shuddered beneath him. Whimpered as he withdrew. Cried out shamelessly as he thrust into her again.

Perspiration swept over his body. He felt hot and feverish with the need of release.

But he held himself back from the climax he frantically wanted. He wanted to keep pleasuring her. Wanted her in arousal state for just a bit longer. She looked so beautiful this way. Beautiful and vulnerable and trusting.

Tucking his hands to each side of her shoulders and keeping his cock buried inside her, he pushed his upper half off her body. Her breasts heaved as she inhaled. He looked down at her flushed face. Her eyes were so bright with need and love that his heart ached from the joy of having her look at him like this. She was so beautiful. Perfection. Sexy.

Too good for him.

Subconsciously he realized the car had stopped and he came awake with one hell of a jolt. With the wakefulness came the intense pain in his upper thigh and a fever raging throughout his body.

It was still dark outside, but through the car window he could see Hannah grabbing and then tossing brush aside. For what seemed an eternity. It eventually dawned on him that a vehicle was emerging from beneath the piles of dead brush.

Fuck! His uncle's old car. It was an antique. A General Chevlectric. Ah yes, the car the slaves knew was missing but had kept quiet about it. They would be safe in this vehicle unless someone had told his uncle about the missing car since Jacob'd left the plantation.

A drop of cold sweat dripped into one eye and he blinked it away.

Man, he was tired. Looking down at his upper thigh, he noticed the dark pool of blood glistening along the edges of the black laser burn in his pants. He wondered if he was still bleeding. Wondered if he would die from the wound. He had no antibiotics to treat himself if it became infected. Couldn't go to the hospital or doctor for he was now a fugitive. And by the shitty way he was feeling he knew he was already in trouble.

Behind Hannah he could see the streak of dawn brightening the eastern horizon.

Would this be the last time he ever saw a morning?

He shook his head, trying to gather his scattered thoughts.

No, he wouldn't die. He had Hannah now. He had something to live for. He would fight death.

A moment later her shadow appeared in his window. She opened the door and held out her hand, much in the same way he'd held out his to her when they'd first come to the motel.

He placed his hand into her palm and tightened his fingers around her flesh, loving the warm soft feel of her.

She smiled down at him. The smile didn't quite reach her eyes and he could see the anxiety there. She was understandably worried.

"We have to hurry. I heard on the communicator they're not far behind us," she said as she helped him stumble from the car through the tall grass to the other vehicle.

He could barely stand. Could hardly get to the car, and when she eased him into the open doorway he fell onto the seat like a lump of log. He was able to get his good leg in, but when she helped him bring the wounded one inside, pain flared, taking his breath clean out of his lungs. Blackness hovered at the sides of his vision and for a moment he swore he passed out and came to again when she was in the driver's seat and starting the car.

"If we can hit the highway before they come down this rural road, we'll be able to merge with the morning traffic. Does Simon know this car is missing from the barn?"

"Your friends covered for you. He has no idea. The car was accounted for as far as I know up until I left. I didn't tell anyone it was missing."

He heard her sigh. Found himself sighing also. They just might make it out of here after all. That is unless the familiar red and green strobe lights of the hit cars came down the rutted road before they got out of here.

He focused his attention to the winding rutted road in front of them, wincing as dry branches screeched against the sides of the car like shrieking prairie dogs. A moment later they erupted from the dirt road to see a moderately busy highway streaming in front of them.

She was moving the car at a fast pace and he noticed the large dip in the road that came between them and the highway.

"Brace yourself," she warned.

Instead of slamming on the brakes, which he'd expected her to do, she slapped her foot onto the electric pedal, bringing a renewed burst of power that flung the car forward at a frantic pace. His stomach hollowed out as they drove into the dip, and of course with his luck the gully contained a large pothole, which she promptly hit. In an instant he was tossed against the side of the car, bringing a fresh round of pain shooting into his leg. The pain pissed him off and once again he fought the black vultures threatening to sweep away his vision. He knew she was panicking. Knew if she concentrated on something else besides the panic she'd be okay.

"Just don't do anything stupid like coming to my rescue again," he warned between gritted teeth.

Through a sweaty haze of pain he noticed her hands tighten around the steering wheel and an angry blush of red sweep across her cheeks. Her bangs lifted in a flurry and her straight hair swept behind her head like a black wave as her head snapped sideways to look at him.

Oh she looked properly pissed at his comment. The panic disappeared and her green eyes sparkled with irritation. In her anger her nostrils flared prettily.

"With thanks like that, don't expect me to."

Despite the throbbing pain in his thigh and the intense fever beginning to cascade through him, he couldn't help but chuckle.

"You're very pretty when you're mad, Hannah. I can't wait to see your face flushing with pure pleasure when I'm thrusting deep inside you."

Her surprised gasp made him smile. He settled back against the passenger seat of the car as they thankfully came up the side of the dip and onto the shoulder of the plastic-paved highway. In a moment the bumpy ride became smooth as silk as she merged in the traffic.

They were safe. At least for now.

Satisfaction gnawed through him.

She hadn't protested what he'd just said. Was she warming to the idea of him making love to her? If so, it was a damn-good incentive to get himself better in one hell of a hurry.

THE FIRST THING JACOB noticed the next time he woke was he didn't feel as if he were on fire anymore. And to his shock, he wasn't in the car either.

Instead, he was lying on a cushy mattress in the cozy attic room of the abandoned mansion Hannah had sequestered while she'd stayed here.

He knew where he was because he'd stolen into this very room the morning he'd found the place. He'd pictured her sleeping in this bed. Smelled her scent on the sheets. Had imagined how her nude body would be splayed out for him on the bed. The desperate hunger for a taste of the sweetness she harbored between her legs had grown with every passing minute. He sensed she was near. She had to be.

Then while looking out the attic window he'd seen her standing down by the beach.

And what had followed would be seared into his memory forever. Going down on her on the beach. Later, in the meadow, he came so close to grabbing her and pushing her over the hood of the car and fucking her senseless it had been almost unbearable not to do it. It had been that kiss of betrayal that almost made him lose his control.

Jacob's shaft hardened at the memory of the intoxicating kiss.

The movement of his erection against the blanket covering him caught his attention. His gaze traveled over his healthy bulge and he found himself looking toward the foot of the bed.

Frilly white sheer curtains hung at the sides of the half-open octagonal window, allowing sunshine and warm salty air to spill inside. To add charm to the rustic white-painted room, a bouquet of fresh-looking yellow buttercups had been stuffed into a dented tin teapot set on the nearby wooden crate.

The roar of the pounding ocean surf drifted into the open window. It barely drowned out the squeaky sound from the rusty windmill perched on the nearby hill.

Other than that, silence permeated the air. It created a bad feeling inside Jacob.

Where was Hannah? Had she left him here? Abandoned him? Taken his uncle's stolen car? Made a mad dash for the border?

He frowned. He hoped she hadn't run again. If one of the slaves eventually did reveal to his uncle his antique electric car was indeed missing and Hannah had taken it, she wouldn't have a chance. She'd be caught. The men at Border Patrol would take her into a backroom, do with her whatever they wanted and then simply kill her. Or if she wasn't lucky, they'd sell her on the black market as a Breeding Slave.

Jacob shuddered at that thought. He'd heard stories about the runaway Breeding Slaves who were unfortunate to get caught by unscrupulous Hitmen or others. The black market paid very well for a Breeding Slave. Those Slaves didn't get access to medical supplies during birthing or given the sexual disease shots all legal Breeding Slaves were required to receive.

He clenched his jaw in frustration. He wished he knew where she was. Wished he could climb out of bed and go looking for her.

But he was so weary. Tired from the loss of blood. He could barely lift his hand to scratch the odd little itch on his nose. He hated feeling so useless.

He tensed at the hollow sound of an approaching car engine and reached for the gun he kept in his shoulder holster. Panic gripped him when he realized he wasn't wearing it.

Or any clothes!

He was a sitting duck lying here. Defenseless. Totally useless. Frantically he visually searched the room and spotted his gun and holster on the night table right beside him.

Cautiously he shifted his body, relieved to discover the pain in his leg wasn't as intense as it had been. He managed to grab the holster and dragged it onto the bed. When he withdrew his gun he heard the door of a car slam. A moment later a second door slammed.

His stomach sank.

There were two of them.

Had they followed Hannah here? Had she left the car outside in plain sight? She was smarter than that. She wouldn't put herself in such danger.

His blood ran cold at his next thought. Maybe she'd been caught and turned him in so she could get a better deal. She was so damn innocent. She could spill her guts all over the place and they wouldn't treat her any better.

She was a Breeding Slave on the run, for God's sake. She had no rights. Didn't she understand that?

Jacob swallowed the tight knot of fear as he heard someone stomp onto the back porch of the mansion two floors down. His heart picked up speed as he heard one set of footsteps climb up the stairs toward the attic.

Toward him!

He'd heard two car doors slam. Was the other person waiting outside?

A floorboard creaked near the top of the stairs.

The urge to lift the blankets over his head and lie as stiff as a corpse was so great he wished he could do it. Instead he unlatched the safety on his laser and placed his finger on the firing button. He would shoot first and ask questions later.

A flicker of movement in the doorway made the breath in his lungs tighten painfully. His finger tightened on the trigger.

Someone stuck their head inside and Jacob almost fired but at the last second caught a flash of brown hair.

"Hannah," he said softly.

She smiled and walked into the room with a duffel bag full of what appeared to be groceries.

"Glad to see you're awake and you didn't kill me." She grinned.

"Where the hell where you?"

"Sweet greetings to you too." She placed the duffel on the bed beside him and placed a cool hand on his forehead. A whiff of her sexy fresh scent drifted into his nostrils, making him very aware of her.

"Where have you been, Hannah?"

"Grocery shopping."

Was she nuts?

"Are you crazy? You've compromised this place."

She frowned. "No one followed me."

"Now you're suddenly an expert on being followed? You didn't even see me watching you yesterday morning."

A teasing glint ripped through her eyes and she asked softly, "Did you like what you saw?"

"I wouldn't be here lying in your bed if I didn't, Hannah," he whispered.

He didn't miss the visible tremor of anticipation zip through her body at his words.

She swallowed and said cheerfully, "Well, obviously you're on the mend. Your fever is gone and—" Before he could stop her, she lifted the blanket covering his wounded thigh. Tucking the softness of the cloth close to his aroused shaft, she draped his erection, keeping it hidden from her view. He had no doubt her eyes would widen with surprise if she saw the full extent of how much he truly desired her.

Cool air drifted against his thigh as she slowly peeled away the white patch covering his wound.

"I must admit I make a pretty good doctor, don't you think?" she asked as she probed gently around the edges.

"A pretty sexy doctor," he muttered.

"Definitely on the mend," she chirped.

And then he remembered that she wasn't alone.

"Who's with you?"

"No one."

"I heard two car doors slam."

"Mercy! Aren't you the paranoid one? I had groceries in the backseat. I'm a little more resourceful than you seem to think I am. We needed supplies so I finally went to town and bought some groceries."

She smiled sheepishly. "I found some money in your glove compartment and used it. I hope you don't mind."

"Anyone recognize you?"

"Would I be here if they had?" she said as she reached for an antique bottle containing some yellowy liquid set on the nearby crate. She squeezed the gooey fluid onto a fresh bandage.

"I put on a wig that I found in an old chest in the basement. Wore a pair of sunglasses and acted natural. No one gave me a second look."

"I'm sure the men noticed you," Jacob mumbled.

She winked at him. "I don't think men would be interested in a gray-haired old woman wearing black clothing and hobbling around with a cane."

"I'd recognize you wearing anything...or nothing."

"Well, obviously you are in no position to find out how I look wearing nothing," she teased.

Jacob inhaled as she placed the cool, ointment-drenched bandage onto his burning thigh. He shouldn't have done that, inhaled that is. He could smell her again. A delicate scent of perfumed soap. It made the familiar need, sharp and deep, wrench through his shaft, hardening him even more.

"Sorry. I didn't mean to hurt you," she said, obviously mistaking his inhalation for one of pain.

"You could never hurt me, Hannah." Unless he lost her.

"I'm glad to hear that because this might be a little uncomfortable." She ripped off some strips from a tape roll and pressed them tight over the bandage and on to his flesh.

He couldn't stop himself from wincing as the pain wrapped around his wound. Nor could he prevent his body from reacting to her sweet, fresh scent.

Boy! If he weren't so damn weak, he'd be taking her into his arms right now.

"There. How does that feel?" she asked as she splayed her hand over the bandage in a soothing manner.

"As long as you keep your hand there, it'll feel good."

He expected her to remove her hand because of his comment and was surprised when she didn't.

Instead, she peered at him with curiosity.

"Why did you put your life in jeopardy to help me escape from that other Hitman?"

Jacob shrugged.

Hannah sighed and shook her head.

"Your picture is plastered all over the newspapers."

"Already?"

"We've been here for three days, Jacob."

Anxiety slashed through him. Three days? How the hell had that happened?

"What?"

"You had a bad fever and I didn't know if..." Her eyes closed and she visibly shuddered.

"You care if I die?" he asked, feeling warm and tingly to know Hannah might want him.

Her eyes popped open. The sight of tears glistening in her green eyes stunned him.

"You saved my life. I owe you."

His happiness vanished. Shit. Of course. He understood. She had only saved his life because he'd saved hers back at the motel by killing Sawblade. She felt nothing but gratitude toward him. He'd been stupid to think otherwise. That knowledge though didn't lessen his desire to be with her and make her his woman.

"I guess we're even then," Jacob replied.

She nodded and pulled her hand off his thigh. Was she suddenly frowning due to the cold way he'd just put it? Or was she frowning because it was true? That she'd only saved him so she wouldn't be in his debt?

"I'll go make you something to eat. It'll give you strength. Before you know it you'll be out of bed."

"I'd rather stay in bed...with you."

Her frown disintegrated and she laughed. "You're definitely on the mend, Jacob. But you'll have to get out of bed in order to catch me."

She moved away and danced out the doorway, blowing him kisses as she went.

"You better make it a good meal, Hannah! Because when I catch you I won't be letting you go."

"Promises. Promises."

Jacob's heart melted at the sound of her laughter as she descended the stairs.

Cripes!

She was going to make him explode with want. He'd better hurry up and get better because if the steely hardness of his aching shaft was any indication, he'd be needing it to change her attitude from laughter to excruciating cries of pure passion.

Chapter Five

IT WAS LATE THAT EVENING when Hannah decided to look in on Jacob one more time before turning in for the night. A good thing too because she caught him trying to wiggle his way out of bed. Fortunately the sheets were so tangled around his legs they were keeping him hostage long enough for her to get to his side.

"Oh no you don't! Do you want to reinjure that wound?" she shouted as she rushed over and pushed him back down against the pillows.

"I need to get out of bed, Hannah. All this lying around is killing me." He sighed in frustration and plopped his head back against the headboard with a dull thud.

"You can't get up yet. Give it another day or two to heal. Until then you're my prisoner and you'll do as I say."

His frown turned into a teasing grin.

"Your prisoner? I like the thought of you doing whatever you want to me."

Hannah couldn't stop the warmth from cascading into her cheeks.

"By the way your face is flushing I think you like the idea too."

She knew she should say something. At the very least deny to him and herself that the thought of him being at her mercy excited her. For the life of her she couldn't acknowledge it out loud. If she did, she'd have to admit to herself she had sincere sexual feelings for him too. The next natural step would be to give him her body and ultimately her heart.

She wasn't prepared to do that. Yet.

She wanted her freedom and he'd made it clear when she'd asked him to run away with her days ago that she couldn't have freedom with him because he had rules he needed to abide by.

Or could they have a future now?

Was there a possibility they could be together? He was now on the run like she was. Both had hits on their heads. Both needed to get out of the country in order to live.

Oh God, dare she be so naïve as to hope they might have a future?

"Hello? Hannah?"

Startled out of her daydream, Hannah looked up to find him staring right into her eyes. Hannah swallowed tightly as he studied her. Where his eyes had been dead days ago they were now alive. Where they'd been cold, they now shone with heat. The transformation looked awesome and a sweet, tingly warmth splashed through her.

"I didn't mean to embarrass you," he said softly.

"You didn't. I only want what's best for you. And right now that means you staying in bed."

"What's best for me is to get out of this bed and get you somewhere safe."

Once again he struggled to get into a seated position.

Despair ripped through her. It was too early for him to get out of bed. What she needed was a distraction.

"Wait! How about if I give you a massage? Will you stay in bed until tomorrow if I give you a massage?"

That did the trick. He stopped struggling.

The pout he'd been favoring yet again vanished. The corners of his sensual mouth lifted into a sexy grin.

Her heart fluttered.

Did he remember? Did he remember how she'd poured the yarrow healing oil onto various parts of his body while he slept? Did he remember how in his delirious state he'd reacted to her touch?

"A massage does sound appetizing."

Hannah detected the lust in his voice and her nerve endings reacted by zipping with anticipation. The thought of touching Jacob's flesh while he was fully awake and aware made her breath back up in her lungs.

"Unless you're afraid of me?" he prodded.

Oh but she was. Afraid of how her body reacted every time she looked at him. Afraid of the way her breasts swelled and throbbed with the need for his touch every time his gaze brushed across them. Afraid of the way her vaginal muscles quivered with an intense hungry ache when she envisioned how much his thick cock would stretch her as he plunged inside her.

"I'm not afraid of you," she found herself whispering, loving the fluttering feeling deep inside her pussy.

He rubbed his hands together in anticipation. "Then let's get down to business. You can start on my legs. They need a good rub down."

He stuck out a very large foot from under the sheets.

"Don't you think my toes are cute?" He chuckled and wiggled his long toes at her.

Hannah laughed, some of the tension easing away from her. She got off the bed and went to retrieve the healing oil. She kept the oil on the crate beside the vase of buttercups she'd picked early that morning.

When she'd brought Jacob here to the mansion three days ago, it hadn't been easy prodding him out of the car and up the three flights of steps. He was delirious from the pain of his wound and weakening by the minute from fever. Despite it being hard to get up to the attic, she figured it was probably the safest place as any since the basement was too damp and cool, and the main and second floors too easily accessible in case someone dropped by.

Hiding in the attic was the perfect spot. There was a hidden trap door that swung the stairs up or down into or out of the ceiling, depending on whether someone wanted to walk up and down. When the stairs were up, all she needed to do was push a bolt to keep anyone from bringing the stairs down. If she was outside, she'd rigged it so the rope was hidden from prying eyes by shortening it and hiding the length beneath a loose ceiling tile.

From inside the attic she could see out the lone octagonal window for miles in either direction up or down the beach, into the ocean and the rolling hills to either side. Another window at the back of the attic allowed her to see if anyone was approaching via the rutted road.

It had been very lucky for her that when she'd first come into the mansion several weeks ago the stairs had been down or she might not have even thought about using the attic to hide. The last user must have left the stairs down so the next would easily find it.

She'd been lucky also in the fact that during Lara's conditioning years her friend had studied herbal treatment in books she found in the school library. She'd taught Hannah a few of those remedies. One of those being the yarrow ointment. Yarrow grew abundantly in a nearby grove yet she had no grease to mix it with.

So she'd set upon trapping one of the many fat rabbits she'd seen hopping around during her previous stay here. Using fishing line and a crate she found in the basement of the mansion she dug up some wild carrots. Placing a crate on the rabbit trail and the carrots beneath the crate, she'd tied the fishing line to the stick which she'd used to prop up the crate. When a fat rabbit had come along, she'd pulled the line. The crate dropped over the creature and, voila, captured rabbit.

She now used the crate as a table beneath the window and the fatty part of the rabbit was inside the jar.

Killing and skinning the creature hadn't been much fun, but she'd needed its body fat for the healing ointment as well as the meat for broth. Using the fat she boiled it with the yarrow, melting the items together over a small fire in a tin pot she'd found.

The herbal ointment had helped heal Jacob's wound and now hopefully with him on the mend they could stay safe long enough for her to convince Jacob to run to freedom with her. Only then could she confide in him that this truly was a contact place for the Underground Railroad.

Hopefully her friend Lara would remain silent about this place should anyone else question her. She suspected the only reason Lara had turned her over to Jacob was because she trusted him. Not to mention the physical attraction Lara had commented many times on between Hannah and Jacob. *If looks could fuck, he'd be fucking you right now*, Lara had laughed on many occasions when Jacob had visited the Breeder Slaves.

If looks could fuck, he'd be fucking you right now. Oh boy, he certainly had that same look as he watched her walk to the foot of the bed with her ointment.

Jacob's gaze followed her every move as she pulled away the sheets, revealing his long, muscular legs. Bunching the covers just above the wound she held her breath and gazed at the leg muscles she'd become intimate with while she'd kept him drugged with her herbal teas. Drugged in an effort to allow his wound to heal. Or maybe she'd kept him doped up because she wasn't yet prepared to allow his promise of making her his own come true?

"They're only legs. They won't bite you," he teased.

The man was maddening. Didn't he know how lethal his legs really were?

She could still remember the silky heat of his muscular thighs as he'd straddled each side of her hips intimately when they'd fallen on the beach after he'd chased her.

"Why don't you sit between my legs?"

Hannah blinked in confusion. Had she heard right?

"What?"

"Sit between my legs. It'll be easier for you to have access to whatever you want...or need."

Was that humor in his voice? Was that dangerous desire glittering in those eyes?

"It's only a massage," he taunted.

Of course it was only a massage. What in the world had she been thinking? The man was as weak as a babe for heaven's sake. All she was doing was trying to distract him for a while with an innocent massage.

Despite telling herself this was all innocent, Hannah's mouth suddenly seemed too dry as she climbed onto the bed and sat cross-legged between his widespread legs.

Avoiding his intense gaze, she poured oil into the palm of her hand.

She began working on his toes, massaging one strong member after another, and then she graduated to one extremely large foot and then the other.

"Hannah, you are heaven-sent," he whispered, his eyes fluttering closed.

Her oil-slicked fingers slid easily over his hot skin and sank deep into the bands of firm muscles lining his calves. She caressed his kneecaps and massaged the tight knots riddling his lower thighs.

Jacob said nothing. His eyes stayed shut, his body in a seemingly relaxed state.

Good.

Relaxed was just the way she needed him. It would keep his teasing words at bay and his sexy gaze from unraveling her.

When she neared the bandaged area on his upper thigh he flinched and she backed off.

"Don't stop," he groaned.

"But it must hurt."

"Nothing I can't handle." A sweet smile lifted his lips and Hannah's heart fluttered. He looked so good when he smiled. He really should do it more often.

Slowly she massaged closer and then peeled away the protective covering she'd placed over the wound. "Looks good. No sign of infection. It's healing nicely."

Pouring more healing oil onto her palm she began massaging the surrounding tender muscles of the red six-inch-long, two inch-wide gash, smiling at the way the tips of his lips grimaced. Obviously she was hitting the right spots. Tonight he'd be sore but in a couple of days his legs would feel brand new with all the tension massaged out of them.

She inched higher and suddenly stopped when she realized the sheets had somehow moved up in such a way that his massive arousal partially peeked out at her.

Hannah gulped at the pleasing sight.

Heavens! No wonder he'd been quiet. He'd been thoroughly enjoying her touch!

"Hannah." She heard the tortured need for release in his voice.

She looked up to see his gaze centered on her mouth, his blue eyes dark with savage lust. The seductive look made her body hum. Made her breathing go ragged. Her heart pound with anticipation.

She almost cried out at the shivers of excitement ripping through her limbs when he lifted the blanket, giving her full view of his unbelievably thick shaft. If she thought he was monstrous while she'd explored his body, as he'd lain helpless in a delirious state, he was massive now.

Her pulse pounded and her mouth watered at the appetizing site. His thick, bulging shaft arrowed toward his belly, the thick plum-shaped head flushing purple with want.

His cock was a seductive invitation. One she couldn't refuse.

"I'll have to be very careful not to reinjure the wound when I tend here." She hadn't realized she'd spoken aloud. The pleasing smile on his face told her she had.

Eagerness roared through her and she poured more oil onto her palms. Lowering her hands over his unbelievably tight testicles, he groaned as she squeezed gently, feeling his swollen balls.

"Breathe deep," she whispered, saying it more to herself than to him.

She began to massage his scrotum. His cock grew visibly harder. Veins pulsed on both sides of his shaft. The head bulged and begged for her attention, but Hannah avoided the area for now. She had another to attend to before coming to rest on her big prize.

After a few moments of gentle pressure on his balls and watching Jacob's eyes darken with lust, her hands left his testicles. Smoothing her fingers over his pubic bone, she rubbed and kneaded him until his breathing deepened and grew hoarse.

Maintaining eye contact, she poured a small quantity of oil onto his shaft. Placing her right hand at the base, Hannah squeezed his cock gently, smiling at Jacob's low growl of approval.

Pulling up along the length of his hard shaft, she slid her hand off the top then immediately replaced her left hand at the base of his penis, doing the same again. Pulling up and sliding off. Right hand. Left hand. Varying the pressure, she took her time and continued to whisper at him to breathe deep.

Then she changed her strategy.

Squeezing the thick cock head as if she were putting it through a fruit squeezer, she then slid her right hand down his entire shaft and off, alternating left and right.

"You do it better than any other woman, Hannah," he murmured.

A wave of jealousy zipped through her at his words. Jacob must have been massaged by many Breeder Slaves that he could say she was the best. But she could do even better, she realized as an idea came swiftly to mind. She couldn't help but smile inwardly. The Breeding Slaves knew of an ancient technique they sometimes used on males whom were selected as their breeding partners. She'd never had the occasion to use the technique but she remembered the instructions very well. If she did this right, she'd have Jacob revealing how he truly felt about her.

Trying hard not to get overly excited at what she was about to do, Hannah leisurely moved away from his aroused shaft and dipped a finger to the area below his tight testicles.

Kneading her finger gingerly along the perineum toward his anus she soon located what she was looking for.

"Breathe deep and slow while I tend to your Sacred Spot."

"Sacred Spot?" Confusion etched his husky voice.

"This area here," she said as she pressed against a tiny pea-shaped hollow halfway between his anus and his scrotum. "It may feel uncomfortable at first, but give me a little time and I'll have you feeling very nice."

"I already feel very nice." He grinned and his gaze traveled to his erect penis. Hannah savored the sensations that coursed through her at the thought of how powerful his thrusts might be if he decided to grab her and flip her onto the bed to have his way with her.

Gently she pressed against the slight indentation.

It felt hard. Tight. Tense.

Jacob squirmed against her delicate pressure but Hannah didn't let go.

"How does it feel?" she asked.

"A pressure. Deep inside. It's uncomfortable like you said."

Hannah detected the anguish in his voice, the sparkles of pain in his blue eyes. Despite his distress, she kept on the pressure.

"The Breeding Slaves used to whisper about this area on a man's body. The Sacred Spot stems from an ancient ritual, a lost science from our ancestors. By massaging the Sacred Spot, a man's body may be able to relax in a way he's never relaxed before, allowing certain emotions to come to the forefront, ultimately granting him great physical and emotional release. It's believed many ailments can be cured with this type of massage."

"I get it. No pain, no gain." A little frown worried his forehead.

He bit his lower lip as she increased the pressure, being especially careful not to press too hard on the sensitive spot.

"Another side effect is after a man's Sacred Spot has been massaged, he will experience fantasy dreams for many nights."

He threw her a wobbly smile. "Bring on the fantasies."

"Why fantasize when you can have the real thing?" she found herself whispering.

His aroused inhalation gave her the encouragement she needed to ask more questions.

"The other day in the car just after you'd been shot, you promised you'd take me, Jacob. You promised you'd make me your own in every way a man makes a woman his. Was that the truth? Or am I just another notch in your belt?"

His eyes darkened dangerously and desire curled through her body.

"I've always wanted you, Hannah. From the first time my uncle brought you to the plantation."

"Why? Is it just a physical attraction because of my looks? Or is it more?"

He blinked in surprise at her question.

"What you're asking is do I want to have a serious relationship with you after the thrill of having sex with you is over?"

Hannah could feel her face flame with embarrassment. She half expected him to laugh. Expected him to remind her she had no rights. That she was nothing more than a Breeding Slave to him.

"I'm a killing machine, Hannah. Trained to follow orders. They trained me so damn well I almost killed you the other day on the beach despite my feelings for you. Even before I approached you I had a laser aimed at your heart. I had my finger on the firing button, telling myself I could never have you anyway so why not just get it over with and do what I'd been sent to do and kill you."

"But you didn't."

"I almost did and that's too close."

Beneath her finger his Sacred Spot tensed again. Obviously he had plenty of anger brewing inside him. The same raw anger and frustration she possessed at being trapped in a life in which she had no say.

"We're victims, Jacob. Victims of an oppressive dictatorship society."

"I know all about being oppressed, Hannah. That's just the way it is. There's nothing we can do about it. But I know one thing for certain, I want you to be safe. Safe from the men who make the rules. Safe from me."

His last sentence stunned her. "Why should I be safe from you?"

Jacob's Adam's apple bobbed wildly as he swallowed.

That familiar look of fear clouded his eyes. It was the same fear she'd seen when she'd approached him in the meadow a few days ago.

Hannah's heart began to pound violently. "What are you afraid you'll do to me?"

"I'm sure you've heard the rumors from the other Breeding Slaves."

Hannah shivered with excitement. The rumors. One of which stated he could keep a woman aroused for hours if not days. Another rumor stated he could orgasm over and over again without losing his erection or spilling his seed.

"Are those rumors true?"

"Yes. But you're like a drug to me. I wouldn't be able to control myself. I'd be too rough. I could hurt you. I don't want that."

Hannah's pulse roared.

"You could never hurt me. I know that in my heart. Besides, I would like rough and uncontrolled lovemaking from a man I love," she admitted.

He blinked at her answer, obviously stunned at her admission. Understanding flared and she knew he realized she wasn't some delicate flower who would shatter if he fucked her good and hard the way he wanted to.

"If I weren't as weak as I am right now, I'd be pounding into you without mercy, Hannah. Thrusting myself into you for hours and you'd be begging me to never stop, just like the other Breeding Slaves did when I went to them for release."

Heat burned through her body at his sensual admission. Heat as well as an insane thrill to experience what he was telling her. Moisture grew between her legs.

His hand reached down, grabbed her wrist and roughly pulled her finger away from his hot Sacred Spot. His gaze impaled her, preventing her from looking away.

"You've got the answers to what you've been looking for, Hannah. I think it's time you leave my Sacred Spot alone and concentrate on something else. Like saving your energy for the things I've got planned for you."

The threat in his words made her ache to have his arms around her. Made her want his hands to touch her, to roam all over her body. To touch every part of her.

And she wanted to touch him too. To make him see she wasn't afraid of what he wanted to do to her.

"Lucky for you, I don't scare easily. Lucky for me, you're at my mercy," she whispered.

Without warning, Hannah bent over and licked the pulsing head of his giant cock. He was so hard against her soft tongue. Like velvet-encased steel. So hard and so hot. She liked the taste of him. The taste of man. The taste of masculine sex.

He groaned.

The wild sound fueled the desire already engulfing her. Suddenly she wanted to feel his flesh pulse against her lips. Wanted to feel the power of his cock push into her mouth. Grabbing the base of his shaft, she lowered her head.

Opening her mouth wide, she slid the head of his cock past her lips. His flesh felt like velvet-encased steel against her hungry tongue. She liked the feel of his penis, the solid muscle, the power that pulsed inside her mouth.

She liked it a lot.

From the corner of her eye she noticed his gaze had grown even darker. In response, she tightened her lips around his cock, her tongue meeting his bulging tip, mating with it, making him groan again.

She took more of him into her mouth. Her lips caressed his hard, powerful length. Her tongue stroked and slurped his organ, and when the tip of his hot flesh touched the back of her throat, Hannah stopped.

Dangerous desire ripped through her like a roaring fire. She could feel her tight control slipping. She wanted his cock not only down her throat but deep inside her pussy. And she wanted him now.

Jacob tried to hold back the groans but he couldn't do it. Hannah was an expert with her lips. She'd been trained well during her conditioning years. Trained to pleasure a man in ways that would have him aching to spill within minutes.

But he'd trained himself too with the Breeding Slaves he'd grown up with on his uncle's plantation.

Those women were beautiful. They were on birth control when they weren't on a mating schedule and they were easily accessible to a young man who was eager to explore his sexual side.

He'd experimented with the women. Learned how to keep himself turned-on for long periods of time. Trained himself to experience multiple orgasms without ejaculating.

Jacob had always thought having sex with Breeding Slaves was a normal part of life. Hadn't thought anything unnatural about it. However, his ideas began to change once he'd been drafted into the Hit Association and he'd met his friend Tool, a fellow Hitman.

Tool, his roommate during the academy, was somewhat of a history buff. He'd whispered about illegal things. Life before Armageddon. Like the days when all women and men had been free to choose what jobs and partners they wanted. Tool had been the one who encouraged

Jacob to work for the affections of a female and not just go off and satisfy himself with a Breeding Slave whenever the urge hit.

Tool encouraged him to pursue Hitwomen at the school. And Jacob had. He wooed them like Tool taught him. By going out on dates with them. Taking them to dinner, the movies and coffee dates.

Things had gone along quite well until the day he'd come home to visit his uncle and the Breeding Slaves he'd grown up with. The day he'd seen Hannah.

Lovely Hannah with the silky brown hair, the gorgeous green eyes and a succulent mouth that was working wonders on his erection.

He watched her suck on him. Watched the lust twinkling in her eyes as her hot, moist lips clamped over his hard cock. Her mouth stretched over him as she welcomed his length inside.

He inhaled a sharp breath as she hollowed out her cheeks and gave him some extra-strong sucks.

Blades of sharp lightning seared along the length of his shaft and rammed straight into his balls, tightening them into painful knots of need and urging him to ejaculate into her seductive mouth.

Gathering all his self-control, he fought frantically to not give in to his release. He wanted this pleasure to last. He wanted her to make love to his throbbing cock with her succulent lips. Most of all he wanted to be healthy and fit so he could fuck her for days on end until she begged him to stop the lusty torture.

But for now he'd take her any way he could get her. And she was doing a damn fine job with his cock.

Hunger flooded her features and she sucked harder, making him gasp at her desperation. Before long his hips were thrusting upward into her mouth, begging her to bring him to release.

But he wouldn't give in so easily. He'd make her work for a taste of him.

As if sensing he was holding himself back, she sucked harder. Shattering orgasms rippled through his cock and he shuddered beneath her beautiful mouth's onslaught.

Still he refused to come. Refused to give up this excruciating satisfaction of having the woman he'd always wanted actually making love to his cock with her mouth.

She kept up the onslaught for a long time. He rode the oncoming orgasms. Rode them with all his might until he hovered at the brink of insanity. Until perspiration swept across his flesh and his harsh groans split the air.

Finally, he could take the agonizing pleasure no longer. Dragging his hands through her silky hair, he clasped the sides of her head and held her steady.

Warning her he was going to come soon, he was surprised to find the sucking on his dick increase into a wild frenzy.

Damn! Did the woman ever tire?

She sucked harder until she totally destroyed his self-composure. His body tightened, the pleasure too overwhelming.

Finally, he gave in to the pressure and released.

The long column of her graceful neck convulsed as she greedily swallowed his seed. Sexy whimpers filled the air as she kept sucking, kept draining him. Eventually relief swept through him and she finally sucked him dry.

Letting go of her head, he leaned back against the headboard, totally spent and wholly satisfied.

He'd been right about Hannah. She was the only woman for him. The only woman who could shatter his self-control so quickly. The only woman who could spear through the lust he harbored inside him and satisfy his needs.

Best of all he knew in his heart she was the only woman who could bring back the man he'd once been.

Alive and ready to love.

Chapter Six

HANNAH LAID HER HEAD on Jacob's firm stomach and listened to his shaky breathing.

She shouldn't have been so rough on him. But the restrained power zipping through his shaft had challenged her to break that steel hardness. And she'd been well rewarded for her efforts because his cum had tasted absolutely yummy.

A perfect combination of salt and spice. She couldn't wait to taste him again.

Her body hummed with desire. She wanted him bad. But he needed his rest. He needed to recuperate.

"Where is it?" he suddenly asked.

"What?"

"Your dildo."

She blinked in shock.

"I know you have one. Despite it being illegal for Slaves to have toys, I know all the women back at the plantation secretly had one or two stashed away to keep them company in between their sex sessions..." His words faded away and he grinned.

"I...I..." she stammered, feeling her face flush with heat.

"Get it," he ordered.

She found herself nodding.

On trembling legs Hannah retrieved the rubber dildo with balls from where she'd stashed it in its handy container in the tiny attic closet. Mere days ago she'd left it here with a heavy heart, sure she would never see it again.

A strange little smile flittered across his face as he examined it closely.

"Almost as big as me," he said as he continued to examine the dildo.

"Take off your pants and underwear, Hannah. I'm going to punish you for holding illegal toys."

Despite the fact he was ordering her with the firm tone of voice men reserved for Breeding Slaves, Hannah felt strangely thrilled at having to stand totally naked in front of Jacob. And at having him dish out the punishment.

Her heart pounded with excitement as she slowly tugged off her shorts and slid her underwear down her legs.

She stepped out of them and lifted her head to find Jacob's eyes sparkling with desire, his gaze focused between her thighs. The tip of his pink tongue poked through his seductive lips.

She remembered his strong tongue slamming into her wet pussy as she'd lain on the sandy beach—her legs stretched wide open for him, the succulent pleasures ripping apart her body as he'd sipped her wetness.

"Take off your top too," he demanded.

She didn't miss the way his fingers tightened around her dildo. Didn't miss the heated look burning in his dark blue eyes as he watched her. Or the increasing sound of his raspy breathing.

With her breath hitched in her lungs, she peeled off her tank top, allowing her heavy breasts to bounce free into the cool night air.

Jacob hissed sharply between his teeth.

"Come here." The demand was no more than an aroused whisper.

He patted his bare stomach. "Settle your ass here and face me."

"I can't sit on you. You're injured."

"My leg is injured. The rest of me is quite healthy as you've experienced. Besides you aren't that heavy. Now come. Sit here."

Sweet mercy! What was he planning to do to her?

Her heart crashed against her chest and a tinge of uneasiness ripped up her spine but she did as he commanded.

Climbing over him, she nestled her butt onto his muscular belly, facing him. Heat seared through her ass and she tried hard to ignore the blossoming hard-on pressed against her backside.

"Keep your hands at your sides while I look at you."

She did as he ordered and let her arms dangle at her sides. Her hands knotted into frustrated fists and she struggled against the need to run her fingers through the sparse thatch of his crisp chest hairs.

Placing her dildo on a nearby pillow, he reached out and intimately palmed her breasts in his hands. His flesh splashed hot and firm against her, filling her with a great urgency to have him touching her everywhere.

"You are so beautiful, Hannah," he whispered as he gazed into her eyes. His thumbs softly caressed her nipples, releasing carnal sparks of electricity. Within seconds she found herself whimpering with need.

"I've wanted to touch you like this for so many years. I've wanted to fuck you since the first minute I saw you."

"Why didn't you?" Arching her back, she pressed her sensitive breasts against his probing fingers.

He said nothing. His eyes smoldered as he studied her. It seemed as if he were debating whether or not he would reveal his reason.

Suddenly he inhaled a shuddering breath and frowned.

"If a Hitman dares defy the Association by running away with a Breeding Slave, he and his mate would be hunted down and killed. All offspring executed. That's not what I want for my woman or children. If I had come to your quarters and fucked you, I would have wanted more. Wanted you as my wife."

Hannah blinked at him in surprise. He'd been holding back because he feared for her and the children they would have?

"What of the Free States? We can go there. They cannot find us there."

"They've been known to track a Hitman straight up through the Arctic. The Hit Association knows no boundaries. Besides, the Free

States is a lawless land. It would be a harsh life for you. Carving out a homestead in the wilderness in a severe climate. They say it's cold up there. We would have to kill our own food. Grow crops in a short growing season. No motels. No stores. No communicators. Too harsh of a life for you, Hannah."

"And being a Breeding Slave isn't a harsh life?"

She found the now-familiar anger snapping through her like a live wire. Of course he wasn't a Slave forced to endure a man fucking him against his wishes, so he wouldn't understand. Only another Slave would know the full extent of what she meant. Yet she still wanted him to know what she felt.

"Popping out a baby a year for twenty or more years isn't harsh? How about watching your own babies being ripped from your arms year after year? Wondering and worrying about what happened to them."

To her surprise, Jacob smiled. "You are beautiful when you're angry. You are proud and determined and stronger than I thought. That's why I'm drawn to you like a moth is drawn to a deadly flame."

She being the deadly flame of course, she thought sarcastically. How romantic.

"Lean back. Spread your legs. I'll ease your anger and then we can talk some more tomorrow."

"Maybe I don't want my anger eased," she teased, suddenly feeling playful. Suddenly wanting to be pleasured. To forget her anger until they could speak again tomorrow.

She gave in to his instruction and leaned back, allowing his long fingers to slide into her wet vagina where he collected moisture then withdrew and began rubbing his finger against her clitoris.

"If circumstances had been different, I would have made you my wife a long time ago," he continued softly.

"Your wife?" Dare she hope he was telling the truth?

"Yes."

She trembled with excitement at his admission.

"But you never so much as touched me. Never gave me an inkling of how you truly felt, except for being nice to me."

"Believe me I wanted you. I want you."

Jacob's head lowered and she gasped as he took a nipple into his moist mouth. Sucking sounds rent the night air. The probing of his firm tongue and nipping of his sharp teeth produced delightful sensations within her breast.

"I'm glad you found me," she whispered, and arched her back, pushing her breast tighter into his hot face.

His sucking stopped.

Hannah sighed with frustration as he lifted his head. His eyes were hooded with excitement as he leisurely licked his lips.

"I came back for you, Hannah. I came back with full intentions of being the first and only Romero brother to fuck you in the breeding stall. I wanted to impregnate you with my seed. I wanted your first child to be mine. To be ours. I wanted everyone to know you were mine. I was fully prepared to fight my uncle and the others on this. I'm glad you ran away, Hannah. Not because I didn't have to confront them but because you've allowed me to see you as a person and not as a possession as I've been brainwashed by society and my parents to believe."

Lowering his head, she gasped as his lips clamped around her nipple again.

The long, hot fingers quickened at her clit. Moving in erotic circles until hot pleasure spilled through her insides. Within seconds she was arching her hips upward.

She closed her eyes, physically tightening her muscles, fully intent on making herself climax.

"Keep your eyes open, Hannah. I want you to watch my punishment to you for you harboring a sex toy."

Her eyes flew open and locked on to his piercing gaze. Incredible sensations slammed through her body at the mixture of emotions flooding his eyes.

There was tenderness.

Lust.

Excitement.

Caring. Even amusement.

"Spread your legs wider and lean farther back against my legs so I can get a good look at that beautiful pussy of yours."

He'd lifted his knees in an effort to support her and she leaned backward until her back settled against his powerful thighs. She realized he hadn't so much as flinched at moving his wounded thigh. He would be healthy very soon. Healthy and full of power, his body ready to unleash a ravenous hunger for a woman.

For her.

Her heart beat violently against her chest at that thought and at the sight of his fierce gaze zeroing in on her pussy. She could almost feel his eyes caress her clit as he stared.

"Tomorrow I'm going to take you. Make you my woman. Tonight though..." He lifted her sex toy off the nearby pillow and she felt it nudge into her moist opening. "Tonight, I'll show you what it feels like to have a man masturbate you."

He pushed the dildo into her slowly, her vaginal muscles gripping the item with hunger, her hips arching toward him, wanting him to go faster. Wanting him to bring about a quick release.

Unfortunately Jacob had other things on his mind.

She moaned when his fingers touched her left nipple. He twisted the quivering bud until she gasped at the sliver of pain. Then his fingers attacked her other one, twisting and squeezing with tenderness until he heard her cry out.

At the same time he was sinking the dildo deep into her body. Her inner muscles wrapped around it in an effort to suck it in. Yet he continued to go so erotically slow until Hannah screamed out her dissatisfaction.

"I warned you, Hannah. I warned you that you weren't safe with me. I warned you..."

His finger found her clit again and he began a steady, firm rub while he withdrew the toy. At his touches, pleasant sensations zipped through her and Hannah closed her eyes once again.

"Keep looking at me, Hannah."

His command was sharp, making her eyes snap open.

Through heavy lids she watched the hungry look seep into Jacob's eyes as he watched her. A mind-shattering climax took her by surprise, exploding through her body with such a wild intensity she screamed out his name.

Another explosion came, followed by more. They were quick, raw bursts of pleasure. The intensity of them made her cry out. His thrusts grew more forceful, the climaxes slammed into her, leaving her gasping for her breath over and over again.

She grabbed his hips for support, her fingers digging into his muscles.

Heavens! He was destroying her with her own dildo! Fire lanced through her as he switched the finger on her clit with a calloused thumb. The pressure and friction splintered her mind.

Armageddon! He fucked good with a dildo.

"You like what I'm doing to you, Hannah?" he whispered.

She couldn't speak. She was too busy concentrating on the heated pleasure spreading like wildfire through her body.

Her breasts heaved frantically as the orgasms continued. His plunging strokes expertly hit sensitive points on the way in. And on the way out the manipulations of the dildo aroused nerve endings she'd never known existed.

She was lost in a mind storm of incredible sensations she'd never experienced before. Lost in the burning lust he'd unleashed inside her. Lost in the hot need for release.

Her hips gyrated beneath the onslaught. The suctioning sound of the dildo sliding in and out of her flew through the air, mingling with her gasps of joy.

He thrust harder. She moaned. Arched her back. Ached for more of this insanity. Frantically she pressed herself against the fraying thumb that circled her slippery clit in a whirlwind of pressure.

Perspiration splashed over her as one climax after another shattered her mind and tortured her body.

The toy continued to impale her. In and out. Oh-so-incredibly delightful.

"Yes! That's it! Keep coming for me. Keep coming."

Hot juice continued to slide from her and laced the dildo. Suddenly his hands clasped her ass. Lifting her hips upward his head sank between her legs. His burning lips suckled her clit and he sipped greedily of her liquid gift. His incredible suckling sent her headlong into yet another wild climax.

AFTER HER EXPLOSIVE orgasms, Hannah managed to snuggle on top of him as if he were her mattress. She was fast asleep with her head nestled on his shoulder, her face mere inches from his. Her breaths spilled across his cheeks in hot little whispers. Her eyes were closed and a satisfied smile tilted her ruby-red lips.

"You did a fine job, Hannah. A fine job," he said softly, careful not to arouse her from her sleep.

The musky taste of her come remained hot in his mouth and it made him remember the way her face scrunched up in ecstasy as he slid the dildo in and out of her. He'd been fascinated at the sight the large toy disappearing into her. Man! Watching that had made him so excited! Made him imagine sinking into her, stretching into her warmth. Made him imagine how her pussy would wrap around his cock as his thick intrusion forced its way home.

But all that would wait until tomorrow.

For now they would rest.

Gently he drew the warm blankets over their nude bodies and found himself smiling.

"This is just the beginning, Hannah. Tomorrow I will make you mine."

PINK AND GOLD RAYS of dawn spilled over Jacob as he lay quietly in the bed. His body, however, was anything but quiet. As a matter-of-fact it was humming. And he was aroused.

Clenching his fists in frustration, he closed his eyes and remembered last night.

Remembered the way her silky fingers had massaged him.

He'd memorized the sweet scent of her clit. The sexy taste of her tight nipples in his mouth. The seductive sounds of her soft whimpers as he'd plunged the dildo into her.

God, he wanted her more now than he'd ever wanted her. What had she done to him last night? Why had she asked all those curious questions? Why had he answered?

Last night her sensual touches had freed his emotions. Brought out the anger, the frustrations he'd stored inside him. Her touches gave him a glimpse of freedom and it tasted fabulous.

Addictive.

Addictive like Hannah. Last night he hadn't been able to get enough of touching her, of tasting her. He knew he'd be like this once he had her. Knew the moment he and she became sexually active he would never be able to let her go. Call it instinct. Call it love at first sight. He just knew he was head over heels.

Today he wanted more of her.

So much more.

Sharp pain radiated through his thigh as flexed his legs. The pain he could stand and it didn't prevent him from climbing out of bed.

What he couldn't stand was being away from Hannah for a minute longer. The time had finally come to show her how much he wanted her.

HANNAH DIPPED A TOE into the ocean waters and grimaced. Not the best temperature for an early morning bath but she craved to get in to the water and soothe her sore pussy from last night's explosive escapade with Jacob and the dildo. Within seconds she was naked, a bar of soap in her hand and up to her waist in the crashing surf.

The water cradled her pussy with its soothing salty liquid, and when she dunked her head beneath the water, she came up quickly, her breath escaping in surprised gasps. Wow! Talk about a splash of cold water to awaken her senses!

Using the soap, she vigorously lathered her long hair and at the same time kept a careful watch on the brightening silhouette of the mansion perched nearby.

Erosion from the ocean had brought the beach practically up to its back door. The giant stone building looked magnificent as the dawn colors of pink and gold splashed against the cracked and dusty windows.

Although she knew it would never happen, she fantasized about that stone mansion as she did her hair. It would be such a beautiful place to live in. No one would have to know they were here. They wouldn't even have to go to town for food. The surrounding buttercup-riddled fields could be dug up by shovel. She'd found planting tools in a shed in a nearby grove. They could plant enough vegetables to get them through a winter.

The area was teaming with rabbits for meat. And they could fish in the ocean. Fruit could come from the numerous apple and pear trees she'd spotted in the same grove where the tool shed was located.

Hannah smiled and hugged herself.

They could have their own children. Children who were free. Children who could run along the beach, their faces flushed from excitement and tanned from the warm sunshine. Jacob and she could show them how to build sandcastles, play games and teach them as well as her how to read and write.

But before all that, she would ask Jacob to build a small boat and they could sail into the sunset every evening and then come home and make love all night long.

And boy did he ever know how to make love with a dildo.

She could only imagine how it would be with the real thing buried deep inside her.

She shivered at the prospect. She needed to hurry. Needed to get herself ready for Jacob.

Splashing the water onto her head, she rinsed her hair. While she washed the rest of herself she felt the anticipation growing at the thought of finally being with Jacob.

"Good morning!"

Speak of the devil!

"Oh my goodness," she gasped in surprise as she spotted him standing on the beach, barefoot and bare-chested, wearing nothing but a pair of tattered green shorts she'd fashioned out of his uniform pants.

Suddenly unexplainably embarrassed, she instinctively turned her naked self away from him, showing him her back.

"No need for being shy anymore, Hannah. I've seen all of you. Why don't you come on out of there so we can pick up where we left off last night? Or would you rather I come in?"

Hannah shivered with delight at his words and looked over her shoulder just in time to see him take a step forward.

"Don't! You'll get your wound infected, Jacob."

"Then come on out. I want to make love to you," he growled, laughter and lust quite evident and his voice.

Oh God! And she wanted him to make love to her too. But not out here in the ocean! It was too cold!

He took another step forward. Waves crashed against his knees and her tummy hollowed out as he stumbled. Thankfully he didn't fall.

"Jacob, don't do anything foolish. You could reinjure yourself," she warned.

"I'll risk it. Turn around. Let me look at you."

Her heart thumped erratically at his demand. Turning slowly, she allowed him to gaze upon her. Desire sparked his eyes and she saw the bulge between his legs grow larger as it pressed against his tattered shorts.

The thought of his erection sliding inside her took her breath away. Brought a wild, thick heat surging through her blood. She kept her eyes glued to that lovely bulge as she moved through the water toward him.

A moment later he embraced her, his hot mouth melting fiery kisses all over her face and then he whispered in her ear, "When I woke up and found you gone, I realized I never want to wake without you again. The time has come for me to show you how much I truly love you."

At his softly spoken words, she enjoyed the shivers of anticipation roaring through her.

"I know you've wanted to see if those rumors are true." His head dipped down and he kissed the valley between her breasts.

The intimate gesture weakened her, made her breasts heave with her every breath.

"I know you want me inside you, Hannah. I know you'd prefer me over your trusty dildo."

His mouth popped her right nipple into his mouth as if it were a ripe cherry. With his teeth he bit and nipped gently until pain and arousal pierced through her breast, zipping all the way down into her pussy, making her wet with that familiar, ferocious desire she had for him.

He released her nipple and worked on the other one until her breast swelled with desire and she whimpered for relief.

Finally his head lifted.

"Come, I've prepared a place for us."

Taking her by the hand he led her out of the water across the warm sand into a nearby thicket. Tall grass secluded them on three sides, allowing them only the view of the white waves rolling upon the beach and the sparkling blue ocean waters a few feet away.

In the thicket, she spotted a large blanket laid out for them. She didn't miss a closed picnic basket nestled in the tall grass. She'd seen the basket beneath the kitchen sink during her stay here and had never thought it would come in so handy.

"Inside that basket is our nourishment. We're going to need it because what I've planned for you will take a while." His lips caressed her neck with more tiny kisses. Kisses that made her heart flutter with joy.

"Jacob, are you sure you're up to this? I don't want you to reinjure yourself."

"After hearing your moans and whimpers last night while I made love to you with that dildo, you're damn right I'm up to this." His voice sounded so unbelievably gentle, but she sensed the barely restrained control shifting through him.

As they stood on the beach, his hand slid across her waist like a brand and spanned over her belly, making her shiver with a brilliant need for him. A need for him to touch her everywhere.

"Show me how much you want me." Her fingers curled around the waistband of his green shorts.

He inhaled sharply at her touch. His blue eyes glittered with arousal.

"I don't only want you, Hannah. I need to be inside you. I need to feel like a man again."

"And I need to feel like a woman. Fuck me, Jacob. Fuck me now. Take me without mercy. Show me how you make love to a woman."

Her fingers tore at his pants, yanking them down. His thick, swollen shaft sprang free and she wasted no time wrapping her hands around his hot flesh.

She aimed his cock toward her slit, anxious for him to be inside her. Her body demanding to be taken. She brought the thickness to her pussy and then she hesitated.

"There's something I need to tell you, Jacob. Something you need to know."

"You're picking one hell of a time to tell me, sweetie."

His hot lips nibbled on her earlobe, making Hannah's knees weaken.

"You're my first real lover," she blurted out.

Shock and surprise flooded his dark eyes. "What?"

"Your uncle, he has an anal fetish and he's been using me that way, he's never used me..."

His finger pressed against her lips, silencing her.

"Thank you for telling me, Hannah."

"You're not upset?"

"I'll always be upset when I think of him with you. I've wanted to kill him many times thinking of it. Many times I thought I would go mad because I was a coward and didn't do anything. But I was trapped like you, Hannah. But unlike you, I wasn't strong enough to break free."

"You're stronger than you give yourself credit for. You didn't kill me. We're here. Together. Let's make a pact. We'll never think or speak about what's happened in our past again. Today is when our lives begin."

To her surprise his hand wrapped around the wrist holding his penis.

"What you've said changes things. I want your first time with a man to be special."

She cried out in protest as he guided her hand away from his thick erection.

His head bent closer and his warm lips caressed the corners of her mouth until she sparkled with joy.

His mouth moved over hers in a seductive manner, turning her knees to jelly and making her body hum with raw desire. Instinctively she knew once this man made love to her, she would belong to him.

Forever.

A warm hand once again settled over her stomach. His finger delicately prodded at her belly button, immediately igniting a lusty fire inside her. It was something so unbelievably beautiful she wondered if she would be able to stand the rest of what he had planned for her.

He explored her belly button with gentle circular motions, alternating between hard thrusts and delicate stabs, similar to the way he'd driven the dildo into her last night.

Damn if this unfamiliar technique wasn't turning her on higher than a firecracker.

His hot mouth sucked at her lips until she opened them. Instantly his tongue slid inside and clashed with hers, unleashing a firestorm of pleasure that had her whimpering into his mouth. His probing finger withdrew from her belly button and his hands covered her swelling breasts. Massaging her fullness, he shaped them with his palms, tweaking her nipples until they burned and ached beneath his caresses.

She'd forgotten they were still standing on the beach, and before she knew what was happening, he lowered her to the warm blanket and onto her back.

He lay down beside her and curled her into his arms, spooning his heated body against her entire length, fitting his thick cock at her vaginal opening.

She inhaled with excitement at the hunger consuming his eyes. Inhaled his raw male scent and reveled in the strong odor of his lust.

"I'm going to start making love to you, Hannah. Don't be afraid. Just know you're safe with me."

She could barely nod, her body trembled with such a strong need to have him inside her.

His mouth quickly resumed kissing her, concentrating on the curves of her lip. He suckled her there. Suckled and nipped until her mouth was stoked with fire.

His thighs moved and she felt his erection plow past her slippery labia lips as he entered her.

Pleasure centers she never knew existed exploded to life as size stretched vaginal muscles that had never been extended so wide by a man. He hadn't entered two inches when her muscles clamped around his thick cock throwing her instantly into a wild orgasm that left her body quaking and her hips shuddering.

When it was over, she realized Jacob was still sinking his length into her. Her juices gushed around his cock and her muscles quivered around him, welcoming him inside.

At his invasion she felt an insane need to increase this erotic fullness. Arching her hips against him, she moaned as he sank even deeper and her vaginal muscles adjusted to the incoming slow-moving missile.

The smell of her arousal intermingled with the salty air. The roar of ocean waves vanished as she listened to his increasingly harsh breathing. His hot chest flattened her breasts. His heart thumped wildly against her flesh. She could feel her own heart beat, joining his in a foreplay of things to come.

Her body shuddered with fear as he flexed his hips. The movement plunged his cock deeper. He kept filling her and filling her.

She had never dreamed a man could fill her insides so much.

Another orgasm hit and her hips twisted wildly at the onslaught. She cried out at the intensity. Fire screamed through every part of her as his iron cock slid over more pleasure centers.

She convulsed again and again. Finally his cock lodged fully inside her. "I'm glad to see my shaft has already pleasured you. And I haven't even started yet," he chuckled against her ear. He moved his head back just enough so she could see his face. His smile looked oh-so wicked with naughty promises. His gaze filled with lust as he looked deep into her eyes. Into her very soul.

"I'm going to brand your pussy with my cock, Hannah. I'm going to fuck you so much. No man will ever come close to satisfying you like I will. You will belong to me."

His words were spoken with such serious conviction she had no doubt he'd make sure she would never stray. It looked as if she were about to experience another one of those Breeding Slave rumors. Once a Slave had a Romero brother brand her pussy, the woman would never want any other man. She wanted this Romero brother. Wanted him with her heart, body and soul.

"Fuck me, Jacob." She grabbed his shoulders, plunging her nails into the taut muscles in his back, pulling him closer.

Suddenly she felt desperate. Desperate for him to do something. Anything to quench her desires.

Slowly he withdrew his cock and speared back inside. She lost her breath at the ferocity of his power. Her fingernails dug deeper into his muscles and she held on tight as he kissed her again.

His thrusting increased and her muscles convulsed around him.

Ripping his mouth free, he groaned into the air. His thrusts were measured. Deep. Hard. Creating such a firestorm inside her she soon hovered between two worlds.

Reality.

And a fantasy world sparkling with a dangerous pleasure so sharp and brilliant she found herself crying out at its intensity.

Her pussy tightened more around his cock. Squeezed him until his warm gasps caressed her cheeks.

Perspiration popped onto her forehead, her face and her entire body. Her juices dripped from between her legs as he pounded into her. The sucking sound of it spurred him on with feverish, animalistic movements.

The scent of their sex hung heavy around them. It seemed to be an aphrodisiac for him. Seemed to make him thrust harder.

Suddenly her mind shattered. Her body exploded into bliss and pleasure.

He continued to ram into her.

She found herself screaming. Crying out at the fiery sensations rolling over her in excruciating waves.

She could barely catch her breath. Could barely hold on to her sanity. She was going to die from this wondrous pleasure, it seemed so intense!

His animalist grunts continued. She followed the sounds. Tried to keep a lifeline to reality.

Another wild thrust from his hips, bringing his cock searing into her and she found the line yanked away as she fell into the other world. A world of blinding arousal, exhilarating pleasure and an insane need to remain here for as long as she could.

Chapter Seven

THEY MADE LOVE UNDER the blanket of warm sunshine, stopping now and again to quench their thirst and hunger from the water and food she'd purchased in town and Jacob had put into the picnic basket nestled beside them.

When the cool canopy of dusk dropped over them, they gathered their clothing and he led Hannah inside the mansion where she was surprised to see the sheet-draped mattress from the attic laid out in the living room on the main floor.

Obviously he'd dragged the mattress down the flights of stairs so they could have a romantic setting in front of the stone fireplace.

He'd planned everything so well.

From their love nest beside the beach, to the snug mattress in front of the fireplace, to the already-set wood in the hearth.

All he did was light a match and a friendly fire crackled away the chill of the oncoming September night. A moment later they lay on the mattress side by side, staring into each other's eyes.

The intensity of his gaze made her heart leap with joy. Made her wonder how in the world she could ever have lived without Jacob. Or how she'd ever survived not experiencing the super orgasms she'd enjoyed today on the beach as he made love to her over and over again.

Without a doubt she belonged to him now. Body and soul.

"I think I need to check your wound," she said as she reached out and ran her hand along his bandaged thigh. Now that she had him, she wanted to be extra careful she never lost him.

"I think I need to fuck you again," he chuckled in response, grabbing her hand and moving it toward his erect cock.

"I like the sound of that. But first I'll check the wound, Jacob."

"It's fine."

"I'll be the judge of that."

Before he could protest further, she removed the bandages from his thigh and examined the injury.

"It looks a little bit red," she said worriedly.

"I'm sure it'll be fine. Hardly hurts at all anymore. Come lie back down beside me. We'll rest and watch the fire for a little while."

Hannah nodded, excitement once again pounding through her nerve endings as she caught sight of his wonderful erection beginning to grow again. From the looks of it, this would be a very short rest.

Rebandaging the wound, she made it a point to remember to put clean bandages on tomorrow, and lay back down on the soft mattress where he curled her into his warm embrace.

She smiled and snuggled, feeling warm and safe. "I'm glad you're here with me, Jacob."

"I'm glad I'm here with you too. It's given me a break from reality. Given me time to explore my feelings and my fantasies about you." He inhaled a shuddering breath, and that dead look she detested suddenly flashed in his eyes. Her stomach clawed with sickness at the sight. He was about to tell her something she didn't want to hear.

"We're going to have to leave, Hannah. It won't be long before someone comes looking for us here."

Is that all? She sighed in relief.

"I should have told you this earlier but we have to stay here," she whispered, and traced a finger around a cute little laugh line at the side of his left eye. "The Breeding Slaves said this is a contact point with the Underground Railroad. They'll come for us. They'll take us to freedom."

"They're just rumors, Hannah."

"No, they aren't!" Sudden anger snapped inside her. "We're safe here as long as we keep out of sight."

"We've been living on borrowed time. I've decided we're going to leave first thing in the morning."

Her blood ran ice cold. "What?"

"We can walk up along the coastline toward the Free States. We can hunt for food. Find our own shelter along the way. Find some way to cross the border and—"

"Haven't you been listening to me? They'll come for us."

"It's too dangerous to wait any longer."

"I was here for weeks before you found me—"

"We can't wait weeks. What if Lara talks again? What if someone else knows about this place and comes gunning for us? We're sitting ducks. Just like you were when I almost killed you. Had it been someone else who found you then you would be dead. Besides, we have no one we can count on for help. No one can be trusted. You've taught me that if we want things to happen, then we have to make them happen and not wait for help."

"We have each other. That's something, isn't it?" She smiled at him but it felt wobbly and weak. She had figured staying here was their best chance at getting to freedom.

"Yes, we have each other. But we still aren't free."

Of course he was right. They weren't free.

Hannah rested her head on his warm chest and listened to his heart pounding against her ear. His hand sifted through her hair and he cupped the back of her neck, tilting her head upward.

"For tonight our love will set us free," he said, and his lips touched hers in a featherlight kiss before he gathered her into his arms and cradled her against his body. She knew he was upset. She could feel it in the tight way he held her. So tight she feared he would crush her ribs.

But there wasn't anything she could say that would soothe him.

Stark reality had reared its ugly head. They were in danger here. Sooner or later someone would find them. Whether it was a Breeding Slave or Stud in the process of being hunted who came here as she had after hearing rumors it was a safe haven for people who wanted to get to the Free States through the Railroad, or someone looking specifically to kill Jacob and her. Besides, she had no idea if the Underground Railroad people had seen Jacob find her here a few days ago. For all she knew, they could have deemed this place as compromised and no one would come to help them.

Sadness clutched at her heart as reality settled in around her. Jacob was right. They were on their own and if they wanted freedom they would have to go and find it themselves.

That meant tomorrow morning they'd have to leave.

EARLY THE NEXT MORNING, Jacob found Hannah sitting on the back porch. Her lovely body was wrapped in a sheet, her bare legs dangling freely off the edge of the veranda as she watched a butterfly flutter nearby along the morning breeze.

Her hair was messy and windswept, and her cheeks flushed rosy from the cool morning air. She looked so pretty he wanted to push her down onto the veranda, rip the sheet from her body and fuck her senseless.

The severe frown marring her face, however, stopped him. It was a frown that speared pain straight into his heart and made him wish they could stay here at the mansion for a few more days.

He knew she didn't want to leave. He didn't want to go either. So far no one had shown up, but deep in his heart he sensed someone would and it wouldn't be a friend. He shuddered at the thought of losing Hannah. Without her he would be a walking zombie again. He would kill himself before he ever let that happen again.

There was something else to consider. They had no transportation. Last night while Hannah slept, he'd stashed Simon's electric car in a nearby gully and covered it with brush. Not that it would help avoid detection much. They couldn't take the chance in using the vehicle this time around. The Hit Association had unique and sophisticated methods of tracking. Unique forms of torture. It would be only a matter of time before they interrogated Hannah's friend Lara. They wouldn't go easy on her either. Slaves were dispensable when it came to extracting information. It would be only a matter of time before they made their way right to this mansion. He hadn't told Hannah about their tracking and torturing methods. She would only worry too much.

"Morning," he called out.

She turned and smiled when she saw him standing in the doorway. To his disappointment the smile didn't reach those pretty green eyes.

"Morning," she replied.

"I missed you when I woke up. Thought we could pick up where we left off before we fell asleep last night."

"I didn't want to wake you. Have you eaten?"

"Not hungry. How about you?"

She shook her head, turned away and returned her attention to the orange-winged butterfly now fluttering around one of the nearby plants.

Jacob slid a hand over Hannah's warm shoulder and squeezed her tense muscles.

"You okay?"

She nodded, but from the angle of her face, he noticed she wasn't okay. Especially when he saw the sparkling tears in her eyes.

Oh man! The last thing he wanted was Hannah to start to cry. It would break his heart.

He sat down on the veranda beside her and ran his hand beneath the sheet. He stroked the warm, silky flesh at the small of her naked back in a comforting motion.

"We don't have to go right now," he said. "We can wait a little while longer if you want."

Her lower lip trembled. "No, you're right. We do have to go. We have to leave our home."

Our home. Shit. Those two words impacted him with such a warm feeling he could barely breath.

"We'll find another home. Somewhere safer than here."

"I know." A sexy smile tilted her luscious red lips and Jacob's breath slammed up against his lungs.

"But just in case something happens to us..." she hesitated, "I want to feel your arms around me one last time. I want you deep inside me. I want you to make me feel safe for just a little while longer."

Without warning she slipped the sheet off her shoulders and let it fall into a puddle on the veranda. Leaning back on her elbows, she allowed him full view of her curvy breasts.

"Your wish is my command." Jacob's shaft hardened at the sight and wasted no time. Reaching out, he cupped her heavy breasts in each hand, and with thumb and forefinger he twisted each juicy-looking nipple.

He watched Hannah's eyes shut. Listened to her whimpers. They were low, sexy sounds that made Jacob's penis thicken even more.

He twisted her nipples until she cried out and her eyes flew open.

"Keep your eyes open, Hannah. I want you to watch me make love to your nipples."

She blinked. Her eyes were full of arousal and understanding as Jacob's head lowered. He took one of her tight buds into his mouth.

The bead was hot and juicy as he nibbled with his teeth and tongued her areola before clamping his mouth over her breast like a suction cup. Her back arched against him and her whimpers made his erection ache with an intense need to fuck her.

Her breaths became labored and harsh as he continued to suckle. He moved from one breast to the other. An occasional cry ripped through the air as he continued to sink his teeth into her hard buds.

Once in a while he'd stop and look up to make sure she was watching. Her pain-pleasure-filled eyes were dazed but she watched how he worshipped her body.

Then he dove at her breasts again. Twisting her plump nipples between his thumb and forefinger, taking the quivering beads into his mouth and nipping them once in a while just to hear her erotic cries.

By the time he was finished, her nipples were red and quivering, her breasts swollen and heaving with her every breath.

Settling his hand onto her silky belly, he dipped a finger into that gorgeous belly button and felt her surrounding muscles tense. Finger-fucking the button was an area of arousal on a woman that was almost always neglected by men. But not by him. He loved the feel of the warm indentation. Loved the idea that this was where Hannah had been secured in a woman's womb.

It reminded him that he would secure children in Hannah's womb.

He would enjoy making her pregnant. Many times.

He could already imagine how sexy she'd look. Her belly big and round with his child. How hard her silky skin would feel beneath his hands as he cupped her swollen flesh.

During her pregnancy he would make love to her and listen to those sweet, sexy moans as he thrust deep inside her. He'd suck her swollen breasts. And then after the child was born and she was once again slender, he would keep fucking her until she was pregnant once more.

He wanted lots of kids. Lots of little boys and girls of his own who he could teach how to play games, how to hunt and fish. And all the while he'd keep fucking Hannah because she was so beautiful and he loved her so much.

THERE WAS AN ODDLY beautiful look in Jacob's eyes as he finally lifted his mouth from her swelled red nipples.

A look that made love fill her heart.

"What are you thinking?" she asked as his fingers slid away from her aroused belly button and drew a teasing line over her abdomen, across her mons to the outside edges of her nether lips.

"I'm thinking about how much I love to fuck you. And how much I love you. Every time I look at you, my heart swells with something I can't explain. I love looking at you. I love to listen to your voice. I love the way you look at me with so much love in your eyes as I fuck you. I want to find us a safe place to live where no one will dictate to us who we will be and what kind of work we'll do."

Her heart thumped wildly at his confessions.

"And most of all I want to have children with you. Lots of them."

The familiar fear of being forced to produce offspring at an alarming rate ripped through Hannah.

"How many?" she asked cautiously, suddenly uncomfortable with the idea she might already be pregnant by his seed.

"As many as you want."

The hot fingers massaging her clit made her gasp as shards of arousal rippled through her.

"How about six?" he asked.

Her eyes widened in shock and he laughed.

"I'm the one who's going to have to carry the babies, y'know," she said.

"You'll make a beautiful mother. And don't think for one minute you being pregnant will stop me from fucking you, Hannah."

She gasped at the intensity of desire flashing in his eyes and at the finger sliding into her vagina. His words overwhelmed her to the point where she didn't know what to say. How could she deny him children if he felt so strongly about her?

She'd thought about having children. Especially when she'd been surrounded by pregnant Breeding Slaves for most of her life. But she'd also seen the dead looks in the mothers' eyes after their newborns had been taken away.

She'd tried to get used to the idea of producing babies with the Studs. She'd also dreamed about how many she'd have when she was free. She'd always thought along the lines of two babies, maybe three.

But six?

Another strong masculine finger slipped inside her moist pussy, making Hannah instinctively lift her hips to increase her pleasure.

His fingers penetrated deeper. He felt so good inside her. Made her feel so excited at the thought of what he was about to do to her.

But six children? The question dove into her mind again. Strangely enough, the longer she thought about having six children with Jacob, the more she liked the idea.

"I think I could settle with four, maybe five."

"You're a demanding woman," he said as he slid another hot finger into her. "I've only got four fingers on one hand."

Hannah laughed between gasps of arousal.

"I mean five children, not five fingers."

"Oh! Sure I knew that." He grinned, slipped a fourth finger inside her and began to thrust slowly, keeping his eyes glued to her face as if watching for her reaction.

At the same time he continued to massage her ultrasensitive clit.

His head dipped and she looked down to see her cherry-colored nipple slip between his sensuous lips. His warm mouth invoked more waves of sensations through her body. Sharp teeth nipped at her aching breasts and nipples, making her gasp with a combination of pain and pleasure. The pain was quickly extinguished as his tongue swirled over the tender areas he'd bitten.

"And after you give birth, I'll suck milk from your breasts, Hannah," he said as he took her other nipple into his hot mouth and nibbled roughly.

Hannah cried out at the fierceness of his mouth devouring her flesh. His fingers plunged frantically inside her wet vagina and she could feel the juices flowing freely.

The shuddering of an orgasm began as her pussy muscles tightened around his fingers. Without warning he popped her aching nipple out of his mouth and withdrew his fingers from her spasming pussy.

Oh heavens! Why was he stopping?

She watched in bewilderment as he quickly scrambled down the veranda stairs and came around to stand between her legs. Within a split second he dropped his green shorts and she inhaled sharply as his erection appeared quite ready for duty.

The sight of his cock intoxicated her.

"I'm going to fuck you so much now, it'll last you until we get to freedom," he stated.

Without warning he grabbed her by the ankles and slid her a little closer to him until her ass hit the edge of the wooden porch and her legs nestled against his powerful hips. The sight of her long legs spread apart on each side of his hips made a heated anticipation rip through her body.

He reached out and ran a hot finger up along the opening to her clit. Hannah's pussy quivered at his touch.

"I can see you won't be needing any more priming. You're so damn wet for me."

"I'm always wet for you, Jacob."

He grinned at her words. It was a sexy grin that made her heart skip a beat.

"Let's try a different approach this time. Shall we?"

Puzzled yet excited, Hannah watched as he lifted her legs onto his muscular shoulders, hoisting her ass a few inches into the air, giving him easier access to her.

"This looks to be a perfect position," he whispered.

Her heart hammered in her chest as his cock head slid into her.

His blue eyes blazed with passion and his strong hands clasped her hips.

Hannah braced herself.

A split second later he plunged his thick shaft deep into her. As he impaled her, the breath tore from her lungs. Grabbing his bare wrists for support, she dug her fingernails into his skin, ignoring his wince of pain. Instinctively she clamped her legs around his neck and squeezed tight. The movement made more room for him and he dove his cock deeper. It filled her to bursting.

He withdrew in an agonizingly slow movement that left her gasping in earnest as she awaited his reentry. She didn't have long to wait.

He thrust inside her again, reawakening all her arousal centers, creating the violent stirrings of an oncoming orgasm.

He must have felt she was on the edge of a climax because his pumping eased off ever so slightly, keeping her gasping for breath and anxiously waiting for him to bring her to a quick fulfillment.

But she knew she wouldn't get her wish.

He wanted this to last a long time for her. And for himself.

Her grip around his wrists tightened as he continued to pump more slowly.

Deep, long hard strokes that made her whimper with both pain and pleasure.

The strength and torturous slowness of his thrusts were amazing. Her muscles clenched around his hot flesh every time he began to withdraw as if she were trying to keep him from leaving her.

Guttural moans of desire escaped his lips. The sound of it like music to her ears.

The pleasure his thick intrusion created made her forget the sadness claiming her about leaving here. Once they were finished making love they would have to leave. It was as if he were thinking the same thing. As if he wanted to make love to her forever.

Once again he picked up his pace. Shooting his hard penis into her like a piston. His tight balls slapped frantically against her ass, turning her on even higher.

She heard him groan again as he pulled out of her and then slammed back inside.

Every time he entered her his cock seemed to be hotter, thicker, filling her even more than the last plunge.

Desperation began to edge his thrusts. His penis thickened and it shuddered inside her. She knew he was going to climax soon.

Opening her eyes, she watched the arousal flood his features. Perspiration drenched his forehead. Tiny muscles in his tightly clenched jaw spasmed wildly. And the cute way his eyes scrunched as he orgasmed inside her made her heart leap with joy.

But he didn't release.

One of the rumors that had circulated was he'd trained himself to have multiple orgasms without ejaculating.

The rumors had been true. She'd experienced that aspect many times during their lovemaking sessions yesterday and she was experiencing it once again.

His face grew serene as the climax passed. Yet he continued to pump into her, keeping her on the edge of bliss. Making her gasp and whimper at the onslaught of his hard thrusts.

By now Hannah's pussy was totally soaked. She could smell the sweet scent of her arousal drifting all around her. Her pussy clenched his cock, holding him tight inside her as pleasure waves exploded yet again through her body.

This time her body shuddered with an orgasm like no other she'd ever experienced. Stars and blackness hovered at the sides of her vision as wave after violent wave of pleasure swallowed her whole, making her cry out at each impact.

She felt her limbs go weak at the assaulting pleasure. Felt her pussy spasm frantically around his shaft as she sailed away into pleasure land.

From somewhere far away and a long time later she heard Jacob's tense shouts as he finally came inside her, spurting his hot seed deep into her core.

Chapter Eight

"HANNAH!" A ROUGH SHAKING on her shoulder zipped through her sex-induced nap with such fervor she snapped her eyes open and gasped at the fear sparking Jacob's eyes.

He pressed a warm finger to her lips and whispered, "Someone's here."

Horrible shivers ripped away the remnants of sleep.

Grabbing her hand and the sheet, he yanked her off the porch. Her tender feet slapped painfully against sharp rocks but she clamped down on a cry. In one violent jerk he pulled her behind the side of the stone mansion.

It wasn't a moment too soon because the back door creaked open and distinct footsteps clomped across the wooden veranda where Jacob had made love to her earlier.

Her heart hammered violently against her chest as he draped the sheet around her shoulders. From out of nowhere his gun appeared in his hand.

"Who do you think it is?" she whispered through chattering teeth.

He shook his head and said nothing.

Fear etched his eyes. His jaw was clenched tight. A muscle twitched wildly in his cheek. He looked as if he were a man ready to kill. The thought made her shiver. The approaching footsteps made her tremble even harder.

He pressed his hand firmly against her belly, pushing her behind him, protecting her from whoever was now descending the steps.

Hannah held her breath and peered over his shoulder. Her heart stopped the instant she saw a gun attached to a very large hand poke around the corner.

Jacob didn't waste any time. He grabbed the deadly pistol and yanked the intruder into the open.

Within a blink of an eye it was all over.

A dark-haired man clad in the standard army green Hitman uniform lay sprawled on his back in the dust. He blinked wide-eyed in apparent shock as Jacob pressed both the intruder's gun and his own firmly against the man's forehead.

To Hannah's surprise the intruder chuckled. No hint of fear showed in his fudge brown eyes. Nor did he appear concerned at the guns pointed at his head. He acted as if he trusted Jacob not to pull the trigger.

Jacob, on the other hand, seemed to be taking the matter very seriously. Tenseness quivered the muscles in his bare shoulders. Waves of angry heat washed out of him, slamming into Hannah, sending signals of alarm shooting throughout her.

"Give me one fucking reason why I shouldn't pull the trigger, you back-stabbing son of a bitch," Jacob growled.

"'Cause I'm your best friend?"

"You were my best friend, Tool. And now you're a talking corpse. Why did you alert them I wanted the tracker turned off to my vehicle?"

Tool didn't answer. Instead he looked at her with an amusing twinkle in his eyes.

"I take it you're Hannah? I'd shake hands but I'll save the introductions for later."

His gaze swung back to Jacob. The smile drifted off Tool's lips and he said rather seriously, "We need to talk. Privately."

To Hannah's surprise, Jacob nodded and pulled the guns away from Tool's forehead but kept them trained on the man.

"I'll meet you out front."

Tool nodded. In an instant he was on his feet, wiping the dust off his backside as he grinned at Hannah.

"Pleased to meet you, Hannah."

With a burst of energy he ascended the porch stairs and casually crossed the veranda toward the open door. Hannah's heart pounded like a battering ram against her chest as she watched the newcomer disappear into the darkness of the mansion.

"Why in the world did you let him go?"

"If he wanted us dead. We'd be dead."

Grabbing her by the wrist with one hand, he slapped the warm handle of his gun into her palm and curled her fingers around it.

"If something happens to me, don't hesitate to use this. The safety catch is off. I need you to back me up. He tries anything, point the gun at his head and press the green firing button. It's as simple as that."

The firmness in his voice had Hannah nodding obediently.

He grabbed her other hand and pulled her up the stairs and into the cool interior of the mansion.

JACOB'S LEGS TREMBLED as a few minutes later he stepped out the front door into the shadowy overhang with Tool's gun clutched firmly in his hand. Immediately he spotted Tool leaning against the hood of his car, his arms crossed casually over his chest. He looked as if he didn't have a care in the world.

But looks could be deceiving.

Sure, it was strange Tool hadn't come in quietly. Perhaps because he knew Jacob would hear him no matter how he came in. When he heard the soft purr of the car while he'd slept, he'd thought it was a part of his dream. A dream he'd been having of fucking Hannah on the hood of a car in a meadow in the Free States. They'd been happy in his dream. So damn happy he hadn't wanted to wake. But when he heard the car door slam and footsteps clomp up the stairs of the house, he'd popped awake, fully alert.

It was odd that Tool was here in broad daylight. A Hitman usually operated under cover of the night, using his keen night eyesight technology to his advantage as well as using the darkness as an element of surprise to kill his runner. It was also suspicious that he had allowed his gun to be taken so easily.

Tool was one of the best Hitmen in the field. He'd been on office duty monitoring the tracking devices simply because he was recovering from a laser shot he'd suffered when he'd been training a new recruit, a Hitwoman, how to shoot. A Hitwoman Tool had fallen head over heels in lust over, clouding his judgment in safety training with the new recruit, hence him getting shot and getting office duty.

Unfortunately Jacob had taken advantage of Tool being in charge of the trackers and Tool had turned him in. The raw anger of betrayal zinged along Jacob's nerves again, making his heart pound with insanity. Squinting against the harsh sunlight, he surveyed the surrounding buttercup-riddled meadows and hillside for evidence that Tool had brought along a welcoming party.

"I'm alone!" Tool called out when he spotted Jacob lurking in the shadowy alcove.

"You better be. Because if you aren't, you'll be the first one I take down with me."

"You already know I wouldn't have let you take my gun if I didn't want you to."

Jacob's insides shook with indecision. Should he simply kill Tool right now, grab Hannah and get the hell out of here?

Or should he hear what Tool had to say?

He took dead aim at Tool's head and stepped out into the warm sunshine. Keeping the gun lined on his target, Jacob walked the twenty feet until he stood directly in front of him.

"You know why I'm here, don't you?" Tool asked. He didn't so much as acknowledge the gun pointed at his face.

Jacob said nothing but his finger itched on the firing button. If he had to, he'd kill Tool in order to save Hannah and feel no pangs of guilt about doing it.

"Your family has made a deal with the Hitman Association. It's rare but it does happen as you know from your history lessons in the Academy training."

Jacob's guts twisted in agony. "What kind of deal?"

"In exchange for a lot of money, instead of your death you are to be captured alive and to face a prison sentence. They promised me a million green ones if I brought you in alive."

"That all?"

Tool grinned. "You think mighty highly of yourself and that woman in there. I must admit she's quite a good-looking woman. She the one who's been on your mind all these years?"

Jacob had confided in Tool about Hannah but never by name. Tool had told him he was a hopeless romantic and thankfully hadn't kidded him about it any more than that, instead telling him he'd be better off dating free women.

"She's the one."

Tool's grin widened. "Yep, still the hopeless romantic."

Jacob allowed himself to relax a bit.

"Why did you turn me in, Tool?"

Raw pain sheared through his friend's eyes and instantly Jacob realized he'd been wrong about him. Guilt ripped through his guts like a lancing sword.

"I didn't."

"Sawblade showed up—"

"I heard."

"So? What happened? How did they know where to find me if you shut off the tracker on my car?"

"Near as I can figure, when I diverted the tracker system from your car to shadow another Hitman working in the area, I triggered some internal alarm that no one bothered to tell me about. The alarm got picked up. Within minutes of the divert all hell broke loose and I had them up my ass. No time to warn you. They stashed me in isolation. Interrogated me. I told them you'd requested some down time because you'd hooked up with some married woman who wanted to keep a low profile. Anyway, they diverted the tracker back onto your car and sent Sawblade over to the motel to help you with the hit that got away."

"He found us."

"Obviously."

Tool's gaze slid to the bandage peeking out from beneath Jacob's tattered green shorts.

"War wound on your leg." His eyes traveled to Jacob's wrists. To the scratches Hannah had branded him with when she'd dug her nails into his flesh while he'd pounded his aching shaft into her.

"More injuries on your wrists, shoulders and back. Looks like you've had a tough time of it." Tool grinned knowingly.

Jacob flushed with embarrassment.

"The entire Hit Association is turning over every stone trying to find you. Doesn't look good for them that a Hitman and a Breeding Slave hooked up together. I guess you realize what you're doing is a big no-no and that even if you are caught alive and put into prison, someone will get you inside."

Jacob nodded. "What I want to know is who tipped you off we might be here."

"Apparently one of your brothers—Jeremy—is quite cushy with Lara, Hannah's friend. Don't tell anyone I told you that, it's supposed to be a big secret. This infatuation with Breeding Slaves seems to run in your family. Anyway, after she heard you were wounded and you two were together and in serious trouble, she eventually confided in Jeremy that she told you Hannah might be here. At least he trusted me enough to know I wouldn't fuck you over. I would have come sooner but I was being watched like a hawk. I slipped away as soon as I thought it was safe."

The look of hurt on Tool's face when he mentioned his brother Jeremy trusting Tool and not Jacob prompted him to feel even worse about not trusting his friend. But hell, he'd had no other choice. What else could he have thought when Sawblade showed up at the motel.

"I'm glad I finally found you. I've got a plan. You want to hear it?"

His words were spoken so casually it took Jacob a few seconds before it fully sank in that Tool was offering to help them.

Jacob nodded and lowered his weapon.

HANNAH CLUTCHED THE gun tighter as she watched Tool get into his car.

Although she wasn't familiar with weapons, she felt reasonably sure she would have shot Tool had he made the slightest suspicious move. There was no way in the world she would ever let anyone hurt her man.

Poking the gun out a crack in the glass of a dirty window, she'd aimed directly at the man, her finger lodged on the firing button just as Jacob instructed.

The two men had talked for a good twenty minutes. For the first few minutes they'd been very serious. Then Jacob lowered the weapon and Hannah had been tenser than a cat on a hot tin roof as she'd wondered what they were discussing.

The front door creaked open and broke Hannah from her thoughts.

She hurried over to meet Jacob.

"What did he want?" she asked when he stepped into the living room.

To her surprise he grinned. "You know what? You look so damn good I could start eating you on the spot."

He took her into his arms and tried to kiss her, but she quickly shoved him away.

"What the hell is wrong with you? You just let him leave. What did he want? What is he doing here?"

"He's here to help us."

"Bull! He's a Hitman, same as you. He's here to take us in. I'm packing. We're leaving."

"We're staying." His voice sounded so calm, Hannah thought he'd snapped.

"You're insane."

"I like being insane. It's more fun this way." He reached out for her and this time she allowed him to take her into his arms. Once again he tried to kiss her. She turned her head away in defiance.

"What did he want?" she asked coolly. She didn't like being kept in the dark. Not one bit.

"To help us."

"And you believed him?"

"We can trust him. If we couldn't, we'd be dead by now."

"But you said he's the one who turned you in."

"It was a misunderstanding. Right now we've got to pack."

"You just said we're staying."

"We are. But we're going to have to abandon the house. It'll only be for a few hours until Tool comes back for us."

"What's going on? Where are we going?"

"Go upstairs and take only what you need. Hide the rest. Hide it good so no one knows we were here. I'll take care of everything down here. I'll explain later."

The excitement in Jacob's voice was contagious and Hannah headed for the stairs.

"Hannah?"

She turned around.

The teasing smile on his face made her breath back up in her lungs.

"Don't forget the dildo. We're going to need it."

NERVOUSNESS INTERMINGLED with pleasure as Hannah tried hard not to squirm beneath Jacob's arousing touches. He'd brought her down to the same secluded little love nest by the beach that they'd used all day yesterday.

Tall grass swayed lazily all around them, hiding them from view.

He'd also tried to reassure her that for now they were safe.

Hannah, on the other hand, was feeling a tad bit uneasy as she listened to the ocean waves lap gently against the sandy beach, half expecting to hear footsteps of many Hitmen sift through the nearby sand.

Thank goodness the only witness watching what Jacob was doing to her was the warm sun slowly climbing into the blue sky.

He'd already aroused her breasts by sucking them, pinching and biting. And now Jacob had started his seductive finger ministrations elsewhere on her body in an effort to keep her calm.

Well, maybe calm was the wrong word. Occupied might be a better word for it.

His thumb slid erotically over her clit, making her pussy moisten with a powerful need for him. The mini orgasms he created as he gently finger-fucked her were having a damaging impact on the serious conversation she was trying to carry on with him.

"Are you sure you can trust him? Are you sure he won't come back with an entire Hit Squad?" she bit out as a second masculine finger slipped erotically into her wet pussy.

He looked up from where he'd been focusing—between her legs. His eyes absolutely glowed with excitement. "He's going to secure a car for us and some ID so we can cross the border to the Free States."

Shock pushed aside her restlessness. "The Free States? You're kidding? Why didn't you tell me earlier?"

"I had other things on my mind. Like getting you in the mood."

Oh Lord. Tool was going to help them get to the Free States and all Jacob could think of to do was have sex? Another long, hot finger slipped inside her and another small orgasm rippled through her.

Damn him! That felt good!

He grinned. Smoky desire pushed away the excitement in his eyes as he continued to massage her clitoris, making her sizzle with need.

"Tool's going to get us through to safety. You'll see. We can trust him. He's got someone at the border working for him."

It was getting increasingly difficult to concentrate on questioning him with all these mini orgasms ripping through her, but she wouldn't stop this pleasure for the world. She just wished he would put her curiosity and nervousness at ease so she could really get into this lovemaking.

"I don't understand. How can a Hitman have someone working at the border for him?"

"He's got resources, Hannah. I can't tell you any more than that. Not yet. Just know that we can trust him. By now he's spread the word that we've crossed the border. They won't be looking too hard for us anymore. Meanwhile, do you like cold weather?"

"How do you know that he spread the word we aren't in the States anymore?"

"It's part of the plan he outlined to me."

"What plan?"

"Hannah, don't worry about it. Let's just enjoy ourselves. Please?"

"You sound like you're begging."

He chuckled and laughter lines burst out at the sides of his eyes. God, he looked so good when he laughed. "That's because I am. Begging to fuck you. Now you didn't answer my question."

"What question?"

"Do you like cold weather?"

What the heck kind of question was that at a time like this?

"No, why?"

"From what I hear it's cold north of the border and we're going to have to keep each other warm."

"I think I'll learn very quickly to like cold weather."

"Thought you would. You know what?"

"What?"

"I'm really thirsty."

He stopped massaging and withdrew his cream-drenched fingers from her. The fire in his eyes and the sight of his stone-hard cock spearing upward from his body made her need grow so intense she quickly lifted her knees and spread her legs wider, allowing Jacob easier access to her.

"Drink away," she whispered, and wiggled her hips invitingly.

He didn't hesitate. Dipping his head between her legs, his hot breath caressed her moist clit and she almost climaxed on the spot.

"Are you sure we can trust him?" she gasped, realizing she was actually enjoying this seesawing conversation between Tool and sex.

He ran his calloused palms up the insides of her legs, making her groan at the erotic feelings slipping through her. He laughed again, obviously enjoying her reaction.

"I've already said we can trust him more than once. Try not to worry. I'll keep us distracted until we hear back from him. He's going to come through for us, Hannah. I've known him for years. We went to the Academy together and trained together. We were roommates. I should have realized he wasn't at fault with what happened back at the motel. And from what I've seen over the years, when he sets his mind on doing something, he follows through on it. He's good that way."

"So are you," she said softly, meaning he was just as good as the man he was praising.

He said nothing. Instead he dipped his head between her legs and a moment later his warm lips clamped over her swollen clit. She moaned when his tongue dabbed against the opening of her pussy, making her climax on the spot. Pleasure convulsions hit, making her moan yet again and she arched her hips against his face in an effort to get more pressure. Vigorously he sucked and lapped, and within moments her brain splintered and her body shuddered again.

Oh Armageddon! The man had a mouth of a god. The intense way he sucked at her clit made the rumblings of another orgasm begin deep within her.

Suddenly he withdrew.

"Don't stop!" she cried out in desperation.

His head lifted and grinned at her, his mouth glistening with her cream.

"I've got a surprise for you, Hannah. Something very special. But first I want you to get on your hands and knees, legs spread wide, facedown, ass up in the air so I can get a good look at you."

His dark voice wrapped around her in enticing waves. It excited her. Aroused her. At this point she would do anything to get relief from the intense desire he'd unleashed inside her. The man certainly was good at distracting her.

Quickly she got into the position he wanted. Her head down toward the blanket, her ass high in the air, legs spread as he'd instructed.

"I wanted to give you a chance to have some more time to get used to this idea...but because I've put myself in charge of distracting you now is as good as time as any to show you how much pleasure I can give to you."

Was he kidding? Every time he made love to her he brought her such exquisite pleasure she'd never known something like it existed.

From behind her she could hear him stand up. A moment later his large hands smoothed some of the warm yarrow healing oil over her ass cheeks.

"Your ass is so velvety, so beautiful." His words were soft and tender, his warm hands expertly caressing her curves. For a brief instant the last time she'd been with Simon popped into her mind, yet she forced him out of her thoughts. He was in the past. Jacob was her future.

Relaxing herself, she immediately felt the first stirrings of arousal ripple through her as a well-lubricated finger nudged against her sphincter.

"I want to take you, Hannah. I want to take you with the dildo in your pussy and me inside your sweet ass. I want to fill you up like you've never been filled before. Would you like that, sweetheart?"

Her heart thundered against her chest at the thought of being double penetrated. She was glad she'd fallen in love with a man who enjoyed variety in his sex life.

"You're so tight, Hannah," Jacob echoed his uncle's words on the last night she'd been with Simon. Once again she forced his uncle out of her thoughts. It was easier this time around. She would be free soon. Free of his uncle. Free of her past.

"So achingly tight. I can't wait to fuck you. To pleasure you." Around and around his fingers went, creating circles of sensual pleasure wherever he touched. Every once in a while a finger or two or even three dipped inside her anus just a little deeper every time, creating whispers of pleasure with every seductive stroke.

Strange sensations blossomed inside her ass, spreading through her like wildfire. Suddenly she felt the thick head of her dildo press against her vaginal opening. Before she could mentally prepare herself, Jacob impaled her with the dildo in one deep thrust.

The unexpected fullness left her gasping for air and moaning for more. Oh sweetness, it felt good.

Slowly he pulled it back out again. She could hear the suctioning sound as her muscles tried to keep the thick intrusion inside her. Could feel the excited quivers inside her pussy as he slid the dildo back inside.

Soon he was plunging in and out of her and at the same time his cock head probed at her sphincter muscle.

The excitement at being double penetrated was overwhelming. Thrusting her hips backward, she urged him to hurry it up. His teasing chuckle penetrated through her layers of arousal. His playing with her frustrated her and made her a little angry.

"Jacob! Please hurry," she found herself gasping.

She groaned in frustration as the dildo poised at her vaginal entrance.

An erotic grunt ripped loose from Jacob and she gasped as his lubricated member slid slowly into the tight passage of her anus. Immediately she realized this was going to be a different experience than the one she'd had with Simon. Simon had been thin and short. Jacob was long and thick. Being anally penetrated by Jacob was going to be an experience unlike any she'd ever had before. The heat of Jacob's thick cock curled through her ass like a hard poker, creating sparkles of dark agony and sweet pleasures that left her craving for more.

He filled her ass, stretching her muscles with such a sinful desire she threw her head back and cried out at its intensity.

"That's right, Hannah. Enjoy it! Enjoy the sensations." Jacob slipped the dildo into her again, wrenching her into another orgasm. At the same time he thrust his cock into her backside, filling her as she'd never been filled before. Stuffing her with such agonizing and incredible sensations she couldn't help but slip into a dark world. It was a pleasure world that eased away all her fears and filled her with wonderful explosions of sizzling pleasure. A dark world that had her convulsing and her mind shattering into wonderful splinters of love, desire and sensual cravings. If there was a heaven, she swore she'd just found it.

"BANG! YOU'RE DEAD." The masculine voice curled through Hannah's layers of sleep, prodding her awake.

At first she didn't realize the meaning of what had just been said. But when she opened her eyes and saw Jacob's friend Tool looking down at them, a gun held precariously in his hand, panic zipped through her making her bolt up.

The sheet covering her body slipped downward, revealing her breasts to the stranger.

Tool's eyes widened in amusement and with an appreciation that made Hannah blush despite her fear.

Grabbing the sheet, she covered herself. Beside her Jacob was cursing violently as he stared at the gun in Tool's hand.

His friend shook his head slowly as he gazed at them. "You really are losing your touch, Jacob. That's twice I've been able to sneak up on you. I think it's time for you to retire to the Free States."

To Hannah's surprise Tool dangled the barrel of the laser gun from his fingers as if it were a dead mouse then threw the weapon onto the blankets covering Jacob's lap.

It was quickly followed by a package.

"This the stuff?" Jacob asked as he eagerly tore open the package, acting as if Tool hadn't just scared the turnips out of both of them.

"It's all there. You two better get ready to go because there isn't much time. My contact is in place at the border, but only for another two hours. It takes an hour and a half to get there. Grab what you need, I'll wait in the car."

Tool threw Hannah a grin and said, "You take good care of Jacob."

"I will."

"Don't be long."

Hannah nodded.

The instant Tool left, she scrambled out from beneath the sheet. Hurriedly she picked up Jacob's clothes and threw them at him.

"C'mon get dressed. You heard the man."

"How about one more quick fuck before we leave?" He reached out and pulled her down onto his naked length.

His thick penis pulsed between her legs and she couldn't help but be aroused.

"Tool said we had to hurry," she breathed as anxiety intermingled with desire.

"So we'll hurry."

His mouth came down on hers with a desperate need. Hannah moaned as his fingers slipped between her legs to fondle her clit. She gasped into his mouth when his thumb lightly caressed her pleasure nub. She was wet within seconds.

All thoughts of freedom zipped away the moment he entered her.

"SHIT!" TOOL POUNDED the steering wheel of their car as they drew closer to the border patrol gate.

Hannah stiffened in alarm.

"What's wrong?" Jacob asked.

"She's not there."

"Turn the car around." The alarm in Jacob's voice sent icy shards of fear ripping through her. She, meaning the contact Tool was supposed to have in place to let them through without a problem.

"If I do that then we'll never have another chance as good as tonight. Besides, if I turn around now it'll draw attention to us. The IDs are good forgeries but we don't need the extra attention."

Hannah curled tighter against the backseat. Her thoughts tumbled in a waterfall of confusion and fear. She wished like crazy that Jacob were back here with her. Wished he could soothe away the tremors of fear zipping through her.

But he wasn't.

He was up front with Tool.

The grim outline of both their faces as they peeked back at her and told her to remain calm made perspiration form on her neck. A bead rolled down between her shoulder blades.

They drew closer to the Border Patrol.

She managed to inhale a deep breath of the stuffy car air in a desperate effort to keep calm.

It didn't work.

She fought the sudden urge to bolt. She had no business involving Jacob and Tool in her flight for freedom. No right to ruin these two men's lives if they were caught with her in the car.

"Are you okay?" Jacob's soothing voice shattered her impending panic.

She nodded quickly and plastered a somewhat wobbly smile onto her face.

"Atta girl. It'll be over soon."

Jacob returned his attention to the front, leaving Hannah alone with the familiar panic rising inside her again. How in the world had she ever allowed them to help her? They would get killed because of her selfishness and her desire for freedom.

The car rolled to a sudden stop.

She felt like crying and just about jumped out of her skin when Tool lowered the window and a Border Guard dressed in a blue uniform poked his head inside.

"Your IDs please."

Tool, who looked as calm as a cucumber, handed him their new IDs.

The guard, a young man of about twenty, scrutinized the pictures on the Identification cards. ID cards that Tool had secured so quickly for them.

Jacob had told her Tool had risked his life going into Hitman Headquarters to get their official pictures from the files. If they ever got out of the States, she'd owe these two men big time.

Suddenly the Border Patrol guard's dark eyes narrowed and he looked at her.

Her pulse exploded.

Despite trying not to, Hannah tensed. She could feel the cold perspiration dot her forehead. Could feel the bitter taste of freedom slipping away.

The guard studied her until she wiggled nervously in the car seat.

To her surprise he said, "Welcome to the Free States, Hannah."

Tool swore softly and Hannah's stomach did a dramatic flip.

"Why the hell didn't you tell me you were one of us? What happened to Cara? Why isn't she at her post?" Tool hissed.

"She came down with the flu. It's going around. She called into the Railroad for help so they sent me in to take over her spot in Border Patrol."

Hannah blinked in surprise and confusion. These men worked for the Underground Railroad?

Did Jacob know? He didn't seem surprised. Tool must have told him while outlining his plan back at the mansion earlier this morning.

"The two of you are entering the Free States on permanent visas," the guard continued, and handed Tool back the IDs. "Use them wisely."

"Get them the hell out of here." The Border Guard slapped the car door and waved them ahead.

Tool slammed the car into drive. Within seconds he crossed the border and drove into the Free States.

Jacob turned around and she saw concern flaring in his eyes.

"Are you okay?" he asked.

Hannah nodded. Emotions, thick and raw overwhelmed her and she couldn't speak. Instead, she nodded.

"We're free," he said.

He should have been happy, but he looked and sounded tired.

Defiance burst through Hannah. No time for being weary. No time to be scared. Excitement shot through her like a drug as Tool drove along the highway that stretched out like a ribbon in front of them.

"We're free and we're together," she stated.

It seemed as if her newfound enthusiasm was contagious because the tips of Jacob's lips curled ever-so slowly upward as if he were now just realizing that yes indeed they were together.

He shook his head as if in disbelief and then started to laugh.

It was a sweet, hearty laugh that warmed Hannah's heart.

"I love you," he shouted.

Suddenly Tool was cursing as Jacob shifted upward in his seat. Hannah screeched as he climbed over the seat and hoisted himself into the back beside her.

Scooping her into his arms, he held her tight. A fierce love shone in his eyes and she swore she could feel her toes curling.

Then to her surprise Jacob held a glittering gold ring in front of her face.

"Hannah Roberts, will you marry me?"

The question floored her but she recovered quickly. Sharp tears of joy stung her eyes and she nodded as he slipped the ring on her finger.

"I will marry you, Jacob Romero, and I will love you for the rest of eternity."

From the front seat they heard Tool cursing yet again.

A moment later Tool spoke, "The justice of the peace will be our next stop, so you guys don't do anything back there until after you're married. Okay, guys?"

When he didn't get an answer, Tool glanced into the rearview mirror and found the newly freed couple kissing.

Happiness burst through him. He smiled and pressed his foot harder on the gas pedal.

Man, he really loved this job.

Don't miss out!

Visit the website below and you can sign up to receive emails whenever Jan Springer publishes a new book. There's no charge and no obligation.

https://books2read.com/r/B-A-WGQ-DVFO

BOOKS 2 READ

Connecting independent readers to independent writers.

www.ingramcontent.com/pod-product-compliance
Lightning Source LLC
Chambersburg PA
CBHW030230180626
46810CB00008B/3058